"Are you going to ask me into the royal penthouse, Your Highness?"

In a heartbeat time melted, taking Amelia back to a year ago when this man had been her lifeline, her protector...her husband. Her skin prickled with awareness.

His eyes seemed to devour her inch by inch. She could tell he was angry—perhaps dangerously so. She'd seen those veiled blue eyes looking just like that whenever anyone got in his way.

"Please don't call me that."

"What am I supposed to call you then? Not Melanie. That's not your real name, is it?"

"You called me Mellie. That could be short for Amelia, as well."

"Nicknames are a show of fondness. I use them for friends. Doesn't apply in this case."

Well, he certainly had sharpened his tiger's claws during their separation. But she'd be damned if she showed him how much he could hurt her.

Dear Reader,

Once again, Harlequin American Romance has got an irresistible month of reading coming your way.

Our in-line continuity series THE CARRADIGNES: AMERICAN ROYALTY continues with Kara Lennox's *The Unlawfully Wedded Princess*. Media chaos erupted when Princess Amelia Carradigne's secret in-name-only marriage was revealed. Now her handsome husband has returned to claim his virgin bride. Talk about a scandal of royal proportions! Watch for more royals next month.

For fans of Judy Christenberry's BRIDES FOR BROTHERS series, we bring you *Randall Riches*, in which champion bull rider Rich Randall meets a sassy diner waitress whose resistance to his charms has him eager to change her mind. Next, Karen Toller Whittenburg checks in with *The Blacksheep's Arranged Marriage*, part of her BILLION-DOLLAR BRADDOCKS series. This is a sexy marriage-of-convenience story you won't want to miss. Finish the month with *Two Little Secrets* by Linda Randall Wisdom, a delightful story featuring a single-dad hero with twin surprises.

This month, and every month, come home to Harlequin American Romance—and enjoy!

Best,

Melissa Jeglinski
Associate Senior Editor
Harlequin American Romance

THE UNLAWFULLY WEDDED PRINCESS

Kara Lennox

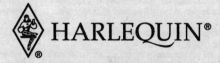

HARLEQUIN®

TORONTO • NEW YORK • LONDON
AMSTERDAM • PARIS • SYDNEY • HAMBURG
STOCKHOLM • ATHENS • TOKYO • MILAN • MADRID
PRAGUE • WARSAW • BUDAPEST • AUCKLAND

Special thanks and acknowledgment are given
to Kara Lennox for her contribution to
THE CARRADIGNES: AMERICAN ROYALTY series.

ISBN 0-373-16917-5

THE UNLAWFULLY WEDDED PRINCESS

ABOUT THE AUTHOR

Texas native Kara Lennox has been an art director, typesetter, advertising copywriter, textbook editor and reporter. She's worked in a boutique, a health club and has conducted telephone surveys. She's been an antiques dealer and briefly ran a clipping service. But no work has made her happier than writing romance novels.

When Kara isn't writing, she indulges in an ever-changing array of weird hobbies, from rock climbing to crystal digging. But her mind is never far from her stories. Just about anything can send her running to her computer to jot down a new idea for some future novel.

Books by Kara Lennox

HARLEQUIN AMERICAN ROMANCE

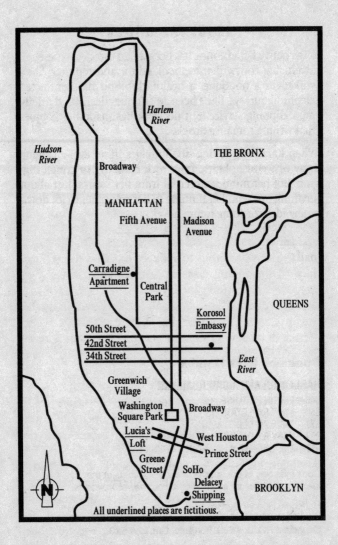

Hudson
River

*Harlem
River*

THE BRONX

Broadway

MANHATTAN

Fifth Avenue

Madison
Avenue

<u>Carradigne
Apartment</u>

Central
Park

QUEENS

<u>Korosol
Embassy</u>

50th Street

42nd Street

34th Street

*East
River*

Greenwich
Village

Washington
Square Park

Broadway

<u>Lucia's
Loft</u>

West Houston

Prince Street

Greene
Street

SoHo

<u>Delacey
Shipping</u>

BROOKLYN

N

All underlined places are fictitious.

Chapter One

"I keep telling you, he's not really my husband."
Princess Amelia Carradigne, granddaughter to the
king of Korosol, didn't even glance up from where
she sat on the window seat in her bedroom, filing her
nails. She was trying to look calm, act calm, in the
face of impending disaster, but her older sister, Cecelia, wasn't making it easy.

CeCe ceased her pacing and leaned down until she
was eye to eye with Amelia. "You said he *was* your
husband, when he called to say he was on his way to
New York."

"I've since consulted our lawyer. The marriage
wasn't legal—no way, no how."

"He obviously means something to you." CeCe
went to the walk-in closet and threw open the door.
"Don't you want to at *least* put on a dress, maybe
some lipstick?"

"Nick has seen me without lipstick. It won't kill
him." Actually, Nicholas Standish had seen her looking a lot worse than she did now. Almost a year ago,
in the former Soviet state of Palemeir, he'd seen her
covered with dirt and bug bites, which was how she
tended to get when she became deeply involved with

a relief effort for the International Children's Foundation. She'd been busy feeding hungry children, doling out medicine and helping them find a safe place to sleep at night. Her own fastidiousness was low on her priority list, even in the presence of the handsomest, most charismatic man she'd ever met.

Amelia abandoned her nail file and turned to look out the window of the penthouse, which offered a magnificent view of Central Park. The city was in the middle of a dreary late-winter rain, but the park still looked inviting even though still wrapped in winter's browns. Amelia wished she could go for a run in that park, just lose herself. She'd rather be anywhere than here, about to face the man she'd lied to, then abandoned.

When Amelia turned back to see what her sister was up to, she was met by a bombardment of clothes. CeCe was pulling dresses out of the closet and tossing them at Amelia.

"Put one of those on. Any of them will do."

Amelia hid a smile as she stripped down to her bra and panties. CeCe, with her sleek, chin-length hair, which she recently dyed reddish-blonde, and her peach silk suit, looked every inch the princess she was—much more so than Amelia, whose curly blond hair was always out of control, and whose wardrobe leaned toward jeans, T-shirts and simple dresses. CeCe's nervous energy made her a whiz in the corporate boardrooms of DeLacey Shipping, where she was second in command to their mother, Lady Charlotte. In Amelia's mind, that was just one step away from running a small country like Korosol.

But Amelia was the princess destined to inherit the throne of the tiny principality nestled between Spain and France. Though CeCe at twenty-nine was older than Amelia by two years, their grandfather, King Easton, had chosen Amelia after CeCe had politely declined the throne. Amelia was both honored and terrified by the prospect, amazed she would be trusted with such an awesome responsibility, and worried she wouldn't live up to the king's lofty expectations.

But she intended to do her best, to earn the trust her grandfather had in her—if this recent scandal didn't cause him to disown her. CeCe's unplanned pregnancy had made tabloid headlines around the world a few scant weeks ago, causing the king a lot of sleepless nights. Fortunately, CeCe had worked things out with the baby's father, Shane O'Connell, and they were now happily married.

Amelia wasn't sure her own scandal would have such a satisfying conclusion. It was entirely possible King Easton would change his mind about his latest choice of heir to the throne. He still had one more Carradigne sister available, twenty-six-year-old Lucia. Though Amelia's younger sister was a free spirit, at least she hadn't stirred up any scandals.

"So why didn't you tell us about Nicholas Standish?" CeCe wanted to know, tugging a dress over Amelia's head as if she were a doll and pulling up the zipper. "I'd have thought you would at least mention it to Ellie."

Eleanor Standish was Nick's younger sister and, proving it was a small world, a member of the king's personal staff who had traveled with him to New York to find an heir among his three granddaughters here. Amelia hadn't even realized Nick and Ellie were related until recently.

"I thought I'd never see Nick again," Amelia said,

finally ending her self-imposed silence about her matrimonial misadventure. "We were desperate. Marrying him was the only way he could get those two kids out of—"

"Oh, yes. Ellie told us about her brother adopting two orphans." CeCe automatically put a protective hand to her tummy bulge, which even her expertly tailored suits could no longer disguise. Pregnancy had softened CeCe around the edges. Once known as "the barracuda," she now melted at the mention of children.

Amelia sighed. "We—Nick and I—ended up responsible for the children after their father died in a foreign embassy blast in Palemeir. Their mother was very sick at the time, and Nick promised her before she died, too, that he would personally care for the kids. But the only way for him to do that was to adopt them. And the only way the Palemeir government would push through the paperwork was if Nick was married. So we got married."

"That's extraordinary," CeCe said, pawing through Amelia's drawers for a half slip and stockings. "I mean, didn't you say he's a mercenary? Such a selfless act doesn't sound like the act of a guy who makes war for money. He must be something."

"He is," Amelia agreed. When she realized how dreamy she sounded, she straightened her spine and frowned. "I'm not wearing stockings."

"So why is he coming here?" CeCe asked, tossing the underthings at Amelia as if she hadn't heard her.

"I have no idea." They'd said their goodbyes at the airport in Palemeir after she'd surprised him by announcing she had to leave right away. The ICF was pulling out, and so was she. But tempted though she'd

been, there was no way she could live as a mercenary's wife in a small town, even if it was in the
country of her heritage. She was destined for bigger
things—like inheriting a throne. Maybe being queen
wasn't her first choice, but it was her duty.

"I'm fascinated by the whole thing," CeCe pronounced. "Not just the secret marriage, but the physical risks you took. I knew you were traveling to dangerous areas, but I didn't picture you right there on
the front lines."

"There were no front lines in Palemeir," Amelia
said. "War was all around us. That's why I was using
the pseudonym, Melanie Lacey, so I could move
around without people gawking or the press interfering with my work."

CeCe brushed an errant curl from Amelia's cheek.
"I know you're not happy the king put a stop to your
activities. But he couldn't allow the future queen of
Korosol to risk her life in war zones."

Amelia understood. But she missed her adventur-
ous life.

Still, she recognized that with the privilege of her
birth came responsibilities, and she was not turning
her back on them.

"What are you going to do with this guy when he
gets here?" CeCe asked, digging through Amelia's
jumble of shoes in the closet. She selected a pair of
white espadrilles, and probably would have shoved
them onto Amelia's feet if Amelia hadn't willingly
stepped into them.

"I don't know that, either." But she'd better figure
it out fast, because the door chimes were ringing im-
patiently.

CeCe dragged Amelia toward the bedroom door. "Come on. I'm dying to meet your Nick."

"Don't call him 'my Nick.' And don't leave me alone with him," Amelia implored.

"No, never," CeCe replied with rippling laughter.

Hester Vanderling, the Carradignes' housekeeper, met Amelia and CeCe at the bottom of the stairs. "Oh, Amelia, there's a gentleman here to see you. I'm not sure how he got past the downstairs security—"

"It's all right. I told the guards to let him in," Amelia said, soothing Hester with a pat on the shoulder. The spry, gray-haired woman was more than a servant. She'd been a part of the family for twenty-five years, serving as nanny to the three Carradigne princesses.

"Is this, um, *the one?*" Hester asked in a whisper. "The not-quite husband?" Hester's feelings had been a bit injured when she learned of Amelia's pseudo-marriage, splashed all over page seven in the *Manhattan Chronicle* by notorious gossip columnist Krissy Katwell. The princesses had always confided all their secrets in Hester, trusting her with things they never would have told even their mother.

Amelia wished now she could get Hester's advice on how to handle the situation. But there was no more time for wishful thinking, because there he was, standing in the foyer, looking even more large and masculine than Amelia remembered, especially with the Carradignes' delicate antiques and pastel silk wall coverings as a backdrop.

"Hello, Nick." Her voice came out a squeak.

"Amelia."

In a heartbeat time melted, taking Amelia back to

a year ago, when this man had been her lifeline, her protector, her hero. Her skin prickled with awareness just at the sight of him, and he'd only said her name.

Once her tunnel vision returned to normal, Amelia realized Nick had the children with him, clinging to him like burrs. What were they doing here? Oh, how she'd hated saying goodbye to them a year ago, almost as much as she'd hated leaving Nick.

Amelia opened her arms. "Josie! Jakob! No kisses for your auntie Mellie?" Jakob, who had to be three now, squirmed away from Nick and ran to her like a friendly puppy. But Josie held back, her blue eyes full of caution.

Amelia gave Jakob a bear hug, smiling warmly at Josie over his head. Josie didn't smile back, her expression carefully neutral.

The expression on Nick's face was anything but neutral. His blue eyes seemed to devour Amelia inch by inch. She could tell he was angry—perhaps dangerously so. She'd seen those veiled blue eyes looking just like that whenever anyone got in his way.

His gaze shifted to CeCe just as CeCe nudged Amelia.

"Oh, excuse me. Nicholas Standish, this is my sister, Cecelia O'Connell. And Hester Vanderling, who practically raised us."

Nick gave CeCe a suitably pleased-looking nod. "Princess Cecelia. Congratulations on your recent marriage."

"Thank you."

"And Mrs. Vanderling." He shook Hester's hand, and she giggled like a schoolgirl. Amelia was amazed Nick had the capacity to be so…so civilized, but she supposed their situation in Palemeir hadn't called for much in the way of manners.

"Who are these cute little munchkins?" CeCe asked, her adoring gaze focused on the children.

"I'm Jakob," the little boy said proudly. "Jakob Standish!"

The corner of Nick's mouth lifted at the mention of his own surname tacked onto Jakob's. The last time Amelia had seen them, Jakob had not been at all sure he wanted to go anywhere with large, gruff Nick, much less accept him as his father. Things must have improved a great deal since then, and all without her assistance. Certainly the children looked better. Jakob's light brown hair had been cropped close, much like Nick's, and his blue eyes sparkled with health. He'd gotten some color, too, and a few more freckles on his nose from being out in the sunshine. Josie's hair, which had been dull and matted in Palemeir, was now a halo of shiny, golden curls.

Amelia felt a pang of regret that she hadn't been part of this almost miraculous transformation and that she hadn't helped the children settle into their new home.

Nick nudged the little girl's shoulder, urging her forward. "This is Josie."

Josie, who would be seven now, held out her hand, which still looked far too thin and delicate for Amelia's peace of mind. "Pleased to meet you," Josie said to CeCe and Hester with perfect manners, then added in a whisper to CeCe, "Are you really a princess, like Cinderella?"

CeCe laughed. "Well, I don't have any glass slippers, and I ride to work in a limo rather than a pumpkin, but I did manage to catch myself a pretty good prince.''

Yeah, rub it in, Amelia thought. CeCe would be living out her own private fairy tale here in America while Amelia was whooshed off to a country she hadn't visited since she was Josie's age, where she didn't even speak the native language.

Life wasn't fair. But then, her work with the ICF had taught her that.

''Josie, you've gotten taller. I think you've grown a foot since I last saw you,'' Amelia said, trying to get the little girl to warm up to her.

''But they both could use some fattening up,'' said Hester. ''I'll bet Bernice has some fresh cookies in the kitchen.''

''Splendid idea,'' CeCe said.

The children looked up hopefully at Nick.

''One cookie apiece,'' Nick said.

Looking delighted, CeCe gave a hand to each. ''We'll be in the kitchen.''

''Traitor,'' Amelia muttered. But she would have to speak privately to Nick at some point. He had yet to tell her why he'd come here, and the sooner he did that, the sooner he would leave. And the sooner he left, the less chance she would make a fool of herself by begging him to smile at her again, to stop making her feel she'd done something criminal.

Even if she had.

Nick put his hands on his lean hips. ''Are you going to ask me all the way into the royal penthouse, Your Highness?''

''Please don't call me that,'' Amelia said.

''What am I supposed to call you, then? Not Melanie.''

"You and the kids all called me Mellie. That could be short for Amelia, as well."

"Nicknames are a show of fondness. I use them for friends. Doesn't apply in this case."

Well, he certainly had sharpened his tiger's claws during their separation. But she'd be damned if she showed him how much he could hurt her.

NICK REFUSED to be impressed by the Carradignes' terrace, where Melanie—*Amelia*—had led him. Apparently there was a spy in or near the household, someone providing tidbits to the gossip columnist, Krissy Katwell, and Amelia thought there would be less chance of someone overhearing their discussion if they went outside.

He hadn't read any New York papers, but the Korosol press had gone to town with the story of the princess's illicit marriage. They'd probably picked up the item from this Krissy person.

Nick had almost fainted when he'd discovered Melanie Lacey was actually Princess Amelia, granddaughter to the king of Korosol. She must have been slumming in Palemeir. Her way of dabbling in charity work. Her little deception had thrown his life into chaos.

Fortunately the rain had stopped. Nick and Amelia sat on opposite ends of a bench in the center of an oasis of trees and shrubs that rivaled Central Park. The greenery sheltered them somewhat from the damp March breeze.

He enjoyed the discomfort reflected on Amelia's face, her stiff, too-regal posture. He wanted to needle her. He wanted to do more than that, after the hell she'd put him through. Unfortunately, he also wanted to bed her. A year's separation hadn't taken the edge off his desire.

A year ago, he'd naively thought a marriage license might afford him that privilege. But once the adoption papers had been filed immediately after their hasty wedding, she'd deserted him.

He wouldn't trust her again. He'd ask for her help, but this time he'd make sure there were no loopholes.

She looked fantastic, he conceded. He'd been half-afraid she would look different in her princess environment, with her hair tortured into some silly style, maybe wearing a tiara and two pounds of makeup. But she was still just Mellie, a natural beauty who required no enhancement. That tumble of gold curls was as unruly as ever, inviting a man's fingers to bury themselves in them. Her green eyes still flashed emerald bright, even out of the intense Palemeiran sun. And her body was just as curvy and luscious as he remembered, more tempting in a casual, flower-sprigged dress.

"So what's going on? Why are you here?" Amelia asked point-blank.

"It's those do-gooders at the Ministry of Family," Nick said. "News of our marriage—and that it wasn't legal—has been picked up in Korosol. The fact you dumped me on our wedding day has brought social workers down on me like a ton of bricks. They say it's obvious the marriage was a fraud, and so was the adoption. Thanks."

Amelia gasped. "They want to take the children from you? They can't!"

"Apparently they can. Korosol isn't America. There's not any legal recourse. The Ministry of Family will investigate, and their decision is final."

"But surely they'll find you're a good father. You're very devoted to those children."

"How would you know? You haven't been around for the past year—a fact that hasn't escaped the social workers' notice. They say we got married with fraudulent intent, adopting children without ever meaning to live as a family. They're old-fashioned in Korosol."

Amelia looked away. "That's my fault, I suppose. But I couldn't stay in Palemeir. The ICF wanted me out of there, and I had to do what they said."

"So you just abandoned your new husband and the children who needed you. Do you have any idea how badly you disappointed Josie?" And him, although he'd shoot himself before he'd admit that to Amelia.

His barb hit its mark. He saw the sheen of tears in her eyes, but she ruthlessly blinked them back. "We both knew the marriage was strictly so you could get the children out of the country," she said. "Even if it had been legal, it *was* a sham."

He intentionally softened his voice. "That kiss at the airport didn't feel like a sham."

Amelia's face turned a flattering shade of pink. She had no ready comeback, and all she could do was look away. He was glad to know that kiss had affected her as it had him. There they'd been, arguing at the Palemeir airport—if one dirt airstrip and a cinder-block terminal could be called that—and suddenly they'd been in each other's arms. They'd never kissed before, not even at their wedding.

That kiss, long and slow and hot, had been everything Nick had fantasized about, and more. He thought he'd won, that he'd convinced her to stay with him. Then he'd realized it was a kiss goodbye.

"I wanted to at least see you and the children to Korosol," she finally said. "But the children were already getting attached to me. It was better that I left when I did. Surely you can see that."

All right, maybe she had a point. There had never been any question that the marriage was one of convenience. He and Mellie had been friends—good, close friends, bonding quickly the way people do in adversity—but nothing more, not that he hadn't wished for more.

They had never discussed a future together, and in fact, what could he have offered her? He was not husband material, and never would be—never again. For that matter, he wasn't really great father material, either. He was no longer capable of fully opening his heart to a child. But in the last year he'd grown so fiercely protective of those kids that he would die for them. Mellie was right about that. Maybe he didn't always say the right thing. Maybe he was too strict. But he refused to let anything bad happen to them—including another major disruption in their home life. He would fight the Ministry of Family with every weapon in his arsenal to prevent them from ripping the kids away from him and thrusting them into foster care.

After a few moments, Amelia was more composed. She sat up straighter, and in a brisk tone, said, "I'd like to help with your situation. What can I do?"

"I would think that would be obvious. You're a princess. Your grandfather is my king, and he's here. Oh, don't look so surprised. I know he is still here, that he didn't return to Korosol after CeCe's wedding. My sister could never keep secrets from me." Nick had tracked Eleanor down in New York, and had figured out that if she was here, so was the king.

"So you want me to intercede on your behalf."

"You get an A."

She looked uneasy, which he didn't understand. The request he'd made of her was simple—far simpler than falsifying marriage licenses and adoption papers.

"Is something wrong?" he asked.

"I'll do what I can, of course. But it's not as simple as you make it sound. First, I'm not exactly on intimate terms with my grandfather. I barely know him. And second, I'm certainly not among King Easton's favorites right now."

"Ah. He doesn't like it when his princesses make the gossip columns?"

"Exactly. And third, he's a stickler for following the letter of the law. He doesn't micromanage his country. Interfering with the Ministry of Family's normal course of business isn't his style."

"You're saying you won't even try?"

"No, I'll give it my best shot. But I think we should see him together, present a united front. It's the best chance we have."

Exactly what Eleanor had suggested.

"We should probably bring the children with us, too," Amelia continued. "It couldn't hurt for Easton to see you all together, as a family."

"Let's do it, then." He stood up, anxious to get his audience with the king over with. The sooner he got this mess straightened out, the sooner he could get his kids back home to the peace and quiet of Montavi, the little mountain town where he was building a new life for himself and the children. And the sooner he could get away from this woman who'd lied to him but still made him tingle in uncomfortable ways.

Amelia laughed. "We can't just walk in on him.

We'll have to make an appointment. Fortunately, your sister is the one who can set it up.''

"I'll talk to her, then.'' Hell, he'd pulled Josie out of school for this trip, thinking it wouldn't hurt her to miss a couple of days of first grade. But now it looked as if she might miss a week or more, and she was already a year behind because of the language problem.

"I'll show myself out.'' He turned and headed toward the terrace doors, wondering where he might find his children in this monstrous penthouse.

"Nick?''

He stopped, turned.

"For what it's worth, I'm sorry I didn't tell you who I really was. But not even the ICF knew my true identity back then. If the truth had gotten out, it could have created a security nightmare. Keeping my identity secret is second nature to me. But you're right, I should have explained before I...before I married you. I didn't think through the possible repercussions, and I'm truly sorry.''

He was surprised by her candor and seeming sincerity. He'd expected her to be different than he remembered her. A year ago, she'd just been a dedicated volunteer who never complained about physical hardships. He'd even seen her give away her own dinner more than once.

He'd had a hard time reconciling that selfless, friendly woman with a Korosolian princess. But now that he'd seen her again, she seemed much the same as before—a fact that was dangerous to his peace of mind. Saying goodbye to her the first time had been torture. And unless he wanted to go through it all again, he'd better harden his heart.

Chapter Two

Amelia had run out of nails to bite as she, Nick and the children cooled their heels in an anteroom at the Korosol embassy. Her grandfather had agreed to see them the day after Nick's arrival in Manhattan, but he'd chosen the embassy as the venue, even though it was Saturday. It was less personal than his quarters at the penthouse would have been—not a good sign. He was treating them like any other subject who wanted his time, but King Easton was not one to give preferential treatment to anyone—not even the future queen.

She had worn her best, most dignified outfit—a gray wool suit with a black silk blouse, silver stockings and gray pumps. She'd even made an attempt to subdue her hair into a tame twist, and at CeCe's urging had actually worn makeup.

Nick, for his part, had cleaned up pretty nicely. He'd been a savagely handsome man back in Palemeir, filling out his camouflage clothes in intriguing ways. His wild, sun-bleached hair, deeply tanned skin and scruffy beard had added to his dangerous image. And Amelia was a sucker for dangerous. She'd always felt smothered by the protective cocoon she'd been raised in—bodyguards, exclusive schools, tinted-windowed limousines. The adventure and excitement of traveling to third world countries under a false identity had held appeal for Amelia as much for the danger as for the chance to help children.

Nick still looked dangerous, but with a sheen of class. He wore a sober suit and tie, the coat taut across his broad shoulders. His hair was a darker blond now, the short, military cut having gotten rid of the sun's highlights. But that didn't stop Amelia from wanting to run her fingers through it, something she'd had to resist since meeting him. She could have ill afforded to fall in love with him a year ago, even less so now.

He was clean-shaven, and his tan had mellowed to a burnished gold. His hands looked strong as ever. She could still see them gripped around his old M16 as he ushered the refugee caravan across a dangerous bridge. But his nails were now clean and clipped neatly.

The children looked adorable, too, in spanking-new clothes, faces scrubbed, hair combed. She hardly recognized them as the same terrified, ragamuffin orphans she and Nick had rescued.

Josie, entirely too somber for a seven-year-old, sat in a wingback chair with her hands folded in her lap, casting cautious glances at Amelia. She was mistrustful of everyone but Nick and Jakob. But the terror of a year ago had left her eyes.

She did not instinctively seek Amelia's comforting embrace as she'd done before. Amelia realized Nick was right—she had disappointed Josie, who had trusted her in Palemeir. Josie showed no outward signs of hostility, but she might never again trust Amelia—a sobering thought.

Jakob, on the other hand, was a little monkey. After thoroughly investigating everything in the waiting room, including some priceless prehistoric artifacts pulled from Korosol caves, he'd crawled into Amelia's lap. A year ago he'd spoken only a few words, but now he chattered like a magpie. He did not remember his birth parents—nor much of anything about his previous life. He did seem to remember Amelia, though, which warmed her heart. She loved children and had always planned to adopt some orphans when she was ready to settle down. The world was just full of children who needed love.

Her status as future queen changed all that. She would not be allowed to adopt, and would in fact be expected to bear a child herself—after she married some stuffy aristocrat. The thought of a loveless marriage "for the good of the country" repulsed her.

"So you really don't know the king?" Nick asked.

"I saw him once in my life before this current visit, when I was a small child. I barely remember it. It's a sore point with my mother—the fact that Easton didn't do something to help her sort things out after my father died, at a time when she needed him most. But I guess he had his own grief to deal with." She paused. "He's grieving now, too. It's been little more than a year since Uncle Byrum died in that terrible jeep explosion."

Nick grimaced. "A terrible thing for Korosol, given what Byrum's death means in terms of succession. I can't think of a man less fit to rule than your cousin."

Nick was referring to Byrum's son, Prince Markus, the apparent heir to the throne since his father's death, though Amelia knew better. For whatever reason,

King Easton did not favor Markus. Since an ancient charter allowed the Korosol king to choose his own successor, Easton intended to do just that.

It would be something of a scandal when he announced that Prince Markus would not succeed him on the throne. Neither would Easton appoint his youngest son, James, a thrice-married Wyoming wildcatter who had proved himself most unsuitable for the throne, not to mention unwilling.

Amelia sighed. "In thinking about the country, though, it's easy to lose sight of the human aspect. The king has lost two of his three sons now. That's the saddest thing, I think, to lose a child."

Nick's face hardened almost imperceptibly. Had she said something wrong? She'd been rattling on, probably because of nerves. Maybe he just didn't like prattling women.

The double doors on the far end of the room whispered open, halting all conversation. Eleanor Standish, Nick's younger sister, appeared. Though Amelia didn't know the king's secretary well, because Ellie had been in America only a few weeks, the two women got along well. Ellie had pitched in to help with CeCe's spur-of-the-moment wedding, proving herself efficient and flexible, not to mention sensitive to CeCe's feelings. Everyone who met her, liked her. However, her frumpy clothes and thick glasses made her look more like a schoolmarm than a trusted member of the royal inner circle.

She certainly didn't remind Amelia of Nick in any way, and Amelia had been shocked a couple of weeks ago when she'd learned the two were siblings. Sometimes it amazed her how truly small Korosol was.

Eleanor and Nick embraced warmly, and the children both ran up with kisses and hugs in abundance for their aunt Ellie. Amelia felt a moment of jealousy that Josie hadn't shown her similar affection.

Ellie studied Nick for a moment. "Nicky. You look very...very civilized."

Nick raised one eyebrow in question. "I don't think I'm being complimented."

"Of course you are," Ellie argued. "I've never seen you in a suit, that's all."

"You've seen me in a dress uniform," Nick pointed out. "That's not much different."

A dress uniform? So Nick had been in the official Korosol military, then. That surprised Amelia. Ellie had said something about her parents disapproving of her brother. Amelia had this impression that Nick had always been a drifter, offering his unique skills to whoever could afford his price. But she supposed he would have had to acquire those skills somewhere.

Nick lowered his voice. "So, how's the wind blowing?"

"With the king?" Ellie thought for a moment. "Hard to say. He wasn't pleased with the quality of his sweet roll this morning. But if anything can cheer him up, these two can. His Majesty loves children. He'll see you now. I should warn you he has another engagement in fifteen minutes, so you'll have to talk fast."

Fifteen minutes. Could they convince the king in such a short time how important it was to keep these children with Nick? How could Easton possibly understand the conditions in Palemeir, the unbelievable risks Nick had taken to honor his promise to Josie and Jakob's mother?

EASTON CARRADIGNE, king of Korosol, threw a handful of pills into his mouth and washed them down with a swallow of bitter coffee just as the door opened to his temporary office and Eleanor entered. She gave him a little curtsy, which she did every time she saw him no matter how many times he told her such an archaic practice was unnecessary. Secretly, though, he enjoyed the gesture of respect.

"Her Highness, Princess Amelia," Eleanor announced. "And Nicholas Standish. Oh, and Josie and Jakob Standish, too."

Easton couldn't believe it. They'd brought the children with them? Did they think he was some doddering, softhearted old man who could be swayed by a couple of moppets?

Well, okay, they were sort of cute, especially the little girl, who moved with such grace and quiet. The little boy, hardly more than a toddler, entered the room like a small hurricane.

"Don't touch that," Easton and Eleanor said together when Jakob tried to peer into the top of a sixteenth-century vase. Nicholas immediately corralled the boy before any harm could be done, and the four of them stood before Easton, waiting for him to acknowledge them. He should have come out from behind his desk to shake their hands, maybe give the little ones some candy, and kiss his granddaughter, the future queen, on the cheek. But he was more tired than usual today. All this business with Amelia's secret, illegal marriage bandied about in the press had worn him out. Especially coming on the heels of CeCe's very public scandal. He hoped Amelia's predicament could be resolved as quickly as CeCe's was.

"You can be seated," Easton said as he took his

own chair—a huge, thronelike thing. Ellie had chosen it for him, and he heartily approved. He relished the pomp and circumstance surrounding his station, even more so these days. Funny how one took so many things for granted until one was about to lose them.

Nicholas and Amelia sat in the wingback chairs that faced Easton's desk. The little boy crawled into Nicholas's lap, while Eleanor fetched a small slipper chair for the girl—what was her name? He'd already forgotten. Was memory loss one of his expected symptoms? Or was he just getting old? Some would say that at age seventy-eight he'd already been old for some time.

Eleanor withdrew, and Nicholas launched right into his statement, which sounded very well rehearsed.

"Your Majesty, I believe my sister, Eleanor, briefed you on the situation here. Princess Amelia and I took on the responsibility of these two children from Palemeir at the request of their dying mother. We married so that I could adopt the children and take them out of Palemeir, where they would be safe."

"What about all the other children?" Easton wanted to know. "Don't get me wrong, I applaud your compassion. Taking on the responsibility for war orphans shows extraordinary generosity. But why these two? You must encounter orphans all the time in your line of work."

"These two were particularly at risk because their father was an American," Amelia explained. "As you know, anti-American sentiments run strong in Palemeir right now. Besides, Nick was with their mother when she died, and he promised to take care of them. He just didn't realize that would mean adopting them—but he is a man of his word."

Easton noticed Nicholas and Amelia exchange a glance. Nicholas ought to be grateful a member of the royal family was pleading his case. But he didn't look particularly grateful. In fact, Easton felt a distinct tension between these two.

"I'm not here to debate Mr. Standish's character," Easton said. "I only want to know the answer to one question. I've asked it before, of Amelia, but she was decidedly unforthcoming. Perhaps you can shed some light on the matter, Nicholas. The Ministry of Family charges that your marriage was a sham from the beginning, that you never intended to live together as husband and wife. Is this the case?"

Amelia looked everywhere but at the king. She seemed to find the wallpaper border fascinating. Nicholas was a bit more direct.

"'Sham' isn't the right word," he objected. "I won't pretend that it was a love match. But I thought Melanie—Amelia—was as committed to the children as I was, and I assumed she would be returning to Korosol with me."

"Melanie?"

"The identity I used when working for the ICF," Amelia said.

"Of course, of course." He'd only recently learned of his granddaughter's alarming activities. Her philanthropic tendencies were to be applauded, but trotting off to war zones was completely unacceptable. He had put a stop to that, posthaste.

"At the time," Nicholas continued, "I thought of the marriage as a temporary solution to a critical problem. Of course, I didn't realize then that my new wife was Princess Amelia. She chose not to reveal that fact to me."

"For security reasons," Amelia added.

"You didn't tell your own husband who you were?" Easton asked, amazed. He was learning a lot about his granddaughters on this trip to America, a great deal of it not very pleasant.

"He wasn't really my husband."

"So the marriage was a sham."

Amelia answered slowly, carefully choosing each word. "I believe Nicholas and I had somewhat different expectations concerning the marriage. In retrospect, I see that I should have handled things differently."

"To say the least," Easton murmured, giving Amelia a hard look. He hoped she would show better judgment when she was queen.

"But it's not fair for Nick to be penalized for my oversight. I'm sure the Ministry of Family is just doing its job, but if their primary concern is for the children, they shouldn't jerk them away from the stable and loving home they've been in for the past year."

"And how, exactly, do you know so much about this stable and loving home?" Easton asked. "Have you been there? Did you observe it firsthand?" Easton knew very well the answer to that question. Neither Amelia nor her sisters had set foot in Korosol in more than twenty years, despite his many invitations. His daughter-in-law, Lady Charlotte, had forbidden it, and because they were American citizens, he had no authority to enforce demands. She somehow held him responsible for the hardships she endured running her family's shipping business after his son Drake's untimely death almost twenty years ago.

Fortunately, his current visit had done much to soften Charlotte's attitude toward him.

"I can tell that the children have been happy with Nicholas because of what I see now," Amelia answered. "A year ago these children were malnourished and practically dressed in rags, not to mention terrified. As you can see now, they're both clean, healthy and well dressed. And they adore Nicholas."

Easton could see the little boy worshiped his adoptive father. He had crawled into Nicholas's lap and was playing peekaboo using Nicholas's tie. The fact that Nicholas didn't participate in the game didn't faze the boy.

The girl, though, worried him. "You, *ma petite,*" he said, pointing to the older child, whose name he still couldn't recall. "How do you like living with Mr. Standish?"

"Uncle Nick is wonderful," she replied solemnly. "He brought us to live in a pretty house in a nice village. We have all the food we want, and I have a pet lamb that Nick says we never have to eat, and we have as many blankets on the bed as we need. He takes me to school every day and he's teaching me French."

"Indeed." Easton was charmed despite himself. The delicate little girl reminded him of his sister Magdalene when she'd been that age, God rest her soul. "And what about the Princess Amelia?" Easton asked. "What do you think of her?"

The child looked taken aback by the question, but Easton was merely trying to get the child away from her rehearsed speech.

"Princess Amelia is very pretty," the little girl

said. "I didn't know she was a princess till Uncle Nick read about her in the newspaper."

"Really?" Easton asked. "What happened then?"

"He got real mad," the girl said matter-of-factly. "He said some words. I think they might have been bad words, but they were in French so I didn't understand them. And he threw a couple of things." She looked over at Nicholas and, seeing his expression of dismay, quickly added, "Oh, but Uncle Nick hardly ever says bad words. And he mostly threw things that didn't break, and he didn't throw them *at* anyone."

Easton chuckled at the child's sober sincerity, then quickly sobered himself. This situation put him into quite a sticky wicket, though it wasn't the stability of Nick's home or the quality of his guardianship that concerned him. Eleanor had told Easton everything he needed to know about her brother's dependability.

"What is it you want from me?" he asked Nicholas point-blank.

"Intervention," Nicholas answered quickly, decisively. "You're the king. One phone call from you and the dragon-lady social workers from the Ministry of Family will drop their case against me and leave me in peace."

"Dragon ladies," Jakob repeated, then giggled.

Easton found nothing to laugh about. This was serious business. He rose from his chair and paced. "I don't think you fully understand what you're asking me to do. Korosol is a constitutional monarchy, not a dictatorship. I've successfully ruled the country for fifty-something years precisely because I don't throw my weight around. The Parliament makes rules, the police and courts enforce them. And I don't go meddling in affairs that aren't my responsibility, no matter what my personal feelings."

"If you don't meddle, and you don't make or enforce laws, what *do* you do?" Nicholas asked with a trifle too much arrogance, Easton thought. But he chose to overlook the breach of protocol.

"I do many of the same things the American president does," Easton explained patiently. "I'm commander in chief of the Korosol Armed Forces. I'm the head of state, and I undertake a number of diplomatic duties. I act as an adviser to Parliament. But I don't run around giving orders. Maybe that's what kings did a hundred years ago in Korosol, but not now."

"So you won't help us?" Amelia asked, incredulous. "Help Nick, I mean. You wouldn't have to issue an order. You could...advise the Ministry of Family, couldn't you? I'm sure they would listen."

"My dear girl, to make requests such as you suggest would open a Pandora's box. Pretty soon everyone would be asking me for personal favors, and many would be as persuasive as you, with causes just as righteous, just as urgent."

"But I'm—" Amelia objected, then stopped herself. He deduced she'd been about to remind him of her newly special status as his successor—as if he needed to be reminded. "I'm your granddaughter," she continued. "A member of the royal family."

"And to alter my standards and ethics just because you're royalty and not some peasant would be even worse. I abhor favoritism under any guise." He turned his attention to Nicholas. "I sympathize with your situation, but it wouldn't be practical for the king to step in and usurp the authority of one of my ministers. I suggest you let the Ministry of Family conduct its investigation. If the situation is as healthy for the children as you say, they'll rule in your favor, without my interference. The Ministry does good work. I have complete faith in it.''

''I'm afraid they won't,'' Nicholas said. ''They've made it pretty clear—no wife, no adoption, no kids.''

Easton felt for this cobbled-together family, he really did. But his hands were tied by his own principles.

A long, awkward silence followed Nick's pronouncement. When it became clear Easton wasn't going to change his mind, Amelia cleared her throat and stood. ''Well, then, I'm sure you have important matters to attend to.''

''We appreciate the audience,'' Nicholas added. ''It's…interesting for an ordinary citizen such as myself to get a firsthand look at how the royal mind reasons out problems.''

Easton had come close to the end of his patience with Nicholas Standish. His veiled sarcasm didn't come close to escaping his notice. A generation ago, men had been thrown into leg irons for lesser insubordination. But Easton knew how upset Eleanor would be if he did anything to her brother, and good secretaries were hard to find. So, again, he let the comment pass.

Nicholas stood and hoisted Jakob onto his hip. He gave Easton a curt nod, then held the king's gaze until Easton nodded back, giving him silent permission to withdraw. The little girl stood last. She said nothing, didn't even look at Easton. But he saw the sheen of tears in her eyes. The silent tears were almost

Easton's undoing, and he knew he would be haunted by her solemn eyes for many nights to come.

NO WIFE, NO ADOPTION, NO KIDS. Those words ricocheted through Amelia's head as Ellie escorted her, Nick and the children down the echoing embassy hallway toward the elevator. Nick's face was hard, impassive, but Josie was blinking back tears. She understood what had just happened. Even Jakob was quiet.

"Come home with me," Amelia said impulsively. "We'll have a nice lunch, and we'll try to figure—"

"No, thanks," Nick said curtly. "The kids and I are going back to our hotel to change out of these clothes, then I'm taking them to the Statue of Liberty. They might as well learn some history while they're here."

Amelia made herself smile at the kids. "That sounds like fun!"

"You can come with us," Josie said cautiously, which pleased Amelia. It was the first friendly overture Josie had made to her.

"No, she can't," Nick said, speaking to Josie but looking at Amelia. "Her Highness can't step out her front door without reporters and groupies descending on her, and I'm not up to dealing with that right now."

Amelia wanted to argue that he was wrong. She could usually move about the city with a certain amount of anonymity, provided she was careful. But she knew an excuse when she heard one. Nick didn't want to be with her.

"When do we go to the orph'nage?" Jakob asked innocently.

"No one is going to any orphanage," Nick said firmly. "Josie, what have you been telling him?"

"But that's where kids go when they don't have parents," Josie said. "Remember that movie we saw, *Annie?*"

"There are no orphanages in Korosol, sweetheart," Eleanor interjected. A bell announced the elevator's arrival, and she gave Nick and the kids quick hugs. "Call me later."

The elevator doors opened, and Amelia started to get on, but Eleanor held her back. "Amelia, I just remembered, I have a...package for you to take home with you."

Ugh. More study materials about Korosol. Amelia hadn't read so much boring material since her last political science class. Nick and the kids boarded the elevator. Jakob waved to her, Josie stared at her, her young face full of disappointment. Nick pointedly ignored her.

Amelia wanted to scream at the ineffectual way she'd handled the situation.

"Come back to my office," Eleanor said. "I don't really have anything to give you. But I wanted to talk to you...about Nicky."

She said nothing else until they were settled in Eleanor's little alcove sipping tea. "How much do you know about Nick's past?" Ellie asked.

Amelia shrugged. "Not very much, really. We became friends in Palemeir, but we never talked about personal things." He'd been easy with her, kind to the children, but she'd recognized an emotional wall when she saw one. There were certain boundaries she'd learned not to cross during their brief acquaintance. One of those was Nick Standish didn't talk about his past.

"Let me show you something." Eleanor reached behind her and picked up a silver-framed photo from a group of personal knickknacks she'd arranged on top of a low bookcase. She handed it wordlessly to Amelia.

The subject of the photo took Amelia's breath away. It was an informal portrait of a family—a beautiful young woman with black hair and dark, dramatic eyes, laughing into the camera; a darling little boy not much older than Jakob, his eyes full of mischief; and a younger, more boyish-looking Nick.

"He was married?" This was something Amelia had a hard time visualizing.

"For five years, very happily. Then Monette and William died in a car accident, about four years ago. It changed Nicky, made him into a different person. He resigned from the army and became a mercenary. He took crazy chances with his life—I believe he didn't care whether he lived or died."

Amelia struggled to absorb this new piece of the puzzle that made up Nick. Now his aura of reckless danger made sense. She'd been drawn to it as much as to his rugged, handsome face and enough muscles for a wrestling team. He and his band of ragtag soldiers had been hired to subdue rebel forces and restore order to the capital city. But somehow he'd gotten caught up in the plight of refugees trying to flee the fighting.

"Those children have changed him," Eleanor went on. "He's not quite the lighthearted, fun-loving man he was before, but I see flashes of the old Nicky beginning to surface. If he loses Josie and Jakob, I don't know what will become of him. A man can only take so much pain.''

''I had no idea he'd suffered such a terrible loss.''

''I wanted to tell you—not because I think there's anything more you can do, but just so you'll understand why he's acting a bit harsh.''

''I don't blame him. I put him in a terrible position. If I'd only realized—''

''Don't blame yourself, either, Your Highness.''

''Please, could you call me Amelia? We've become friends, after all.''

''Yes, but you're soon to be queen.''

Amelia resisted the urge to groan. She detested pomp and circumstance.

''At any rate,'' Eleanor went on, ''I wanted to express my appreciation for what you did to help Nick and the kids. It was a huge risk for you as well, staying behind until the ICF practically dragged you out.''

But it had been an easy choice for Amelia. It might have been a marriage of convenience, but she'd have done anything to protect those children. And Nick— well, saying vows in a church with him at her side had been a little frightening, but a part of her had thrilled at the idea of being married to such a powerful, dangerous man.

If she had it to do over again, she would have stayed with them, returned to Korosol with them and consequences be damned. But she'd made the wrong decision. Now she carried the responsibility of that mistake with her. The fates of those children were on her head, and it was up to her to make things right. But how?

Chapter Three

Macy's opened early on Sunday morning specifically for a private royal shopping party. As Amelia shopped for baby things with her two sisters and Hester, she couldn't get her mind off Nick's dilemma.

No wife, no adoption, no kids.

"Hey, how about this?" Lucia held up a hot-pink romper embossed with psychedelic flowers.

"Mmm, cute," Amelia said absently.

"Cute?" CeCe repeated. "It's ghastly. Even Lucia knows it's ghastly, and she's a bohemian. She was trying to get a reaction out of you, and you aren't paying the least bit of attention. I need your help with the nursery decor."

"I'm sorry," Amelia said. "I'm just a little distracted."

"Poor dear," Hester said, putting her arm around Amelia. "It's that Nicholas, isn't it. You've been blue ever since he showed up. Well, he'll be gone soon."

"That's just what worries me," Amelia said, sinking into a cherry-wood rocking chair. "He believes he doesn't have a prayer with the Ministry of Family. But he's not about to relinquish those kids. I'm afraid he'll do something desperate."

"You mean like kidnap the kids and take them to Canada or somewhere?" Lucia asked, pulling up her own rocking chair.

"Exactly. Nick is a skilled mercenary and survivalist," Amelia said, anxiety building in her chest. "He could slip across any border undetected. But that's no way to bring up children. They need a stable, safe home."

"Stable and safe is overrated," Lucia said, drawing one leg up and resting her chin on her knee. "You've said that yourself a million times."

"Yes, but I'm an adult. With children it's different."

"Children love adventure, too."

Lucia was the real rebel in the family. She lived in a loft in SoHo despite their mother's vociferous objections, crafting avant-garde jewelry in her studio and actually selling it to the public. Charlotte thought it was far too common an activity for a princess, but Lucia was starting to make a name for herself. Her brooches and earrings were showing up on debutantes all over New York, and even a few Hollywood actresses had been seen displaying Lucia's designs.

With her shoulder-length blond hair hanging loose and windblown, and her flamboyant clothes, Lucia looked even less like a princess than Amelia. But the girl had a spine of steel and the will and determination of a charging rhinoceros. Secretly, Amelia thought Lucia might make a very good queen. She would love the attention, at any rate. But Easton had chosen Amelia instead because she was the next in line, and that was that.

"It's a shame dear old Granddad didn't come through for Nick," CeCe said, sitting on the edge of a carved wooden toy chest. "He can be a rigid old goat sometimes."

"Cecelia," Hester scolded. "We don't speak that way about our king." But she pulled up a chair, too, and pretty soon the four of them were deep in conversation, the shopping expedition forgotten. The salespeople and bodyguards all politely withdrew out of earshot.

"I don't understand why this Family Minister or whatever wants to take the kids away from Nick if he's such a good father," Lucia said. "I mean, so he's single. Big deal. Single people in America adopt all the time. And it's not like potential parents stand in line to adopt older children."

"Ministry of Family," Hester corrected. "Korosol isn't America. They're much more traditional and old-fashioned than we are here. But it does seem a shame that a little technicality like lack of a wife should keep Nick from holding on to Jakob and Josie."

"Hey, what if he married someone else?" CeCe asked.

"Yeah, why not?" Lucia said. "A guy like that shouldn't have any trouble finding a wife. He could probably snap his fingers, and a dozen would stand in line."

"He already thought of that," Amelia answered quickly, dismayed at how disturbed she felt at the thought of Nick marrying someone else. "He would run into the same problem he has now. The Ministry of Family is hung up on the fact that Nick got married solely to facilitate the adoption. If he entered into another quickie marriage, it would be obvious what he was up to. So that's not the answer," she concluded, relieved she could argue so eloquently against CeCe's idea. It made her squirm to picture Nick with some other woman—only because she worried that another woman might not care about the children the way she did, Amelia reassured herself.

"Hmm." Lucia tapped her chin, looking thoughtful.

"I just feel so terrible," Amelia said. "It's my fault he's in this pickle. I ought to do something to—what do you mean, 'Hmm'?" Amelia zeroed in on Lucia. Of all of them, Lucia was the most used to thinking outside the box—which made her a constant worry to their mother. But she was also a great problem-solver.

"How badly do you want to be queen?" Lucia asked.

That was a good question. "I want to do it, I guess. It's an amazing opportunity. I'm not crazy about the idea of giving up anything resembling a private life, but I'm willing. Why?"

"I've got an idea—but it might kill your chances with Grandfather."

Oh, dear. Lucia had that look of daring in her eyes that had always gotten them all in trouble when they were kids.

"Well, speak up, girl, what is it?" Hester urged.

"Amelia, why don't you simply marry Nick—for real, nice and legal?"

Amelia's heart hitched at the very thought before reality reasserted itself. She threw her hands up in the air. "Oh, for heaven's—"

"No, no, wait, hear me out," Lucia said. "This is good. By marrying Nick and readopting the children, you prove to the Ministry of Family that you really were serious back in Palemeir, and it was just circumstances that separated you. You solve Nick's problem."

Lucia's suggestion met with stunned silence for a few seconds. Then CeCe spoke up. "And she also renders herself ineligible for the throne. I mean, a queen can't marry an ex-mercenary and adopt children. Right?"

"Nick is a handsome devil," Hester added. "If I were a few years younger and didn't have my Quincy, *I'd* marry him."

"Yeah, not a bad bonus, getting to share a bed with him."

"Lucia!" Amelia felt the heat rising in her face because her sister had voiced exactly what she'd been thinking. "You've never even met him."

"Yeah, but CeCe told me he was hot."

"I said he was handsome," CeCe objected.

Amelia laughed. "You all can't be serious...can you?"

Three pairs of eyes looked expectantly at her.

"But he's furious with me. He would never agree to it."

"From what you've said," CeCe pointed out, "Nick would do whatever it took to keep those kids."

Amelia had to concede that was true.

"Anyway, it's not like you have to stay married the rest of your lives," Lucia pointed out. "Once the Minister's Family is convinced the marriage was genuine after all, they'll turn their attention elsewhere, and you and Nick can quietly divorce."

Amelia gave her younger sister a friendly shoulder nudge. "Trying to get rid of me so *you* can be queen?"

Everyone laughed at that. "Grandfather dearest

isn't about to hand over his precious country to me,'' Lucia said. ''Not after the spectacle I made of myself at CeCe's wedding.'' She was referring to the fact that she'd shown up at the sumptuous society wedding on the arm of a rock singer. ''He'll have to look elsewhere for an heir to the throne. I mean, we're not his only grandchildren. There's always Cousin Markus to fall back on.''

Amelia shook her head. ''I'm not marrying Nick. Mother would have a fit. She wants one of us to be queen so she can play Queen Mum.''

That produced another round of laughter. Charlotte wasn't the Queen Mum type. She had her own empire to run—DeLacey Shipping. But she did want to keep peace with the king now that they were somewhat reconciled, and she did hope for great things for her daughters. She would be terribly disappointed if Amelia sabotaged her chance to inherit the throne of Korosol.

For the time being, discussion of Amelia marrying Nick was put on the back burner, for which she was grateful. The four women launched themselves into shopping in earnest. But one phrase kept running through Amelia's mind…

No wife, no adoption, no kids.

When they arrived back at the penthouse, arms laden with sacks and boxes for the nursery, Bernice, Charlotte's rotund, rosy-cheeked cook, enticed the sisters to have lunch before they all went their separate ways. Charlotte joined them. Amelia had hoped her grandfather, who was staying at the penthouse, might also venture out and share in the meal. In a more informal setting, she might broach the subject of Nick and Josie and Jakob again. But he took his meal in his room, which he often did.

Charlotte presided over lunch as if it were a board meeting. Her slim stature, erect posture and short, tousled white hair made her look far younger than her fifty years. She was deeply concerned about her girls' futures, but she had spent so much time away from her daughters when they were young that none of them felt terribly close to her.

"So, Amelia," Charlotte began as they all munched on crab-salad croissants around a table on the screened lanai, "how did Mr. Standish's audience with the king go?"

"That was yesterday," Lucia commented. "You're just now asking?"

"I've been busy," Charlotte said tightly. "We've got the dock workers threatening to strike and a new ship to ready for dedication next week. The mayor's coming for that one, you know."

Lucia poked her fork into the crunchy end of her croissant. "I thought you were interested in Nick's audience."

"I am, of course. And I'm sure Amelia will tell me what happened, if you'll stop sniping at me."

"Sniping? All I did was—"

"Knock it off, Lucia," Amelia said wearily. "You were picking a fight and you know it." Lucia and Charlotte mixed about as well as gasoline and matches. All of her life, Amelia had been the peacekeeper. If it wasn't Lucia trying to establish her independence, it was CeCe trying too hard to compete with her mother, though Charlotte had been getting along better with CeCe since learning of her impending grandchild. Charlotte, who had not been the most attentive of mothers while the princesses were growing up, intended to make up for it with her grandchildren.

"You're right," Lucia said grudgingly. "Sorry, Mother."

Charlotte smiled at Lucia. "My little drama queen. You always did like to scrap. I've always had that problem myself." Crisis averted, Amelia related to her mother what had happened during Nick's brief audience.

"He can be so inflexible," Charlotte said in an exasperated reference to the king. "And once he's made up his mind, there's no changing it."

"I was afraid you'd say that." Amelia blotted her mouth and set her napkin on the table, no longer hungry. She couldn't just stand by and do nothing. She had to at least talk to Nick one more time. He'd avoided her and all of the New York Carradignes like Ebola ever since their audience yesterday. She'd pried the name of his hotel out of Eleanor, and left half a dozen messages, but he wouldn't return her calls.

Each hour that passed with no word from him increased Amelia's suspicion that he was going to do something crazy. And she was powerless to stop him.

Or was she?

Quincy Vanderling, Hester's husband, opened the door and stepped onto the lanai. "Begging your pardon, ladies," he said even as he grabbed an olive off Amelia's plate and popped it into his mouth. He then smoothed his thinning white hair in a gesture of nonchalance.

When Hester had come to America to work for Lady Charlotte and Prince Drake shortly after their marriage, a besotted Quincy had followed, eventually hired as the Carradignes' butler—and as Hester's husband. Slightly stooped and a little husky, he wasn't very butlerish. But he was utterly devoted to Hester and the Carradigne family.

"What is it, Quincy?" Charlotte asked.

"Miss Eleanor Standish is here. She needs to deliver some faxes to the king, but she would like to pay her respects to you all as well. Want me to put her in the Grand Room?"

Ellie! Exactly who Amelia needed to see. She popped out of her chair. "I'll bring her out here. Maybe she'll want a sandwich—there's plenty of crab salad left."

Amelia wended her way through the kitchen and up the back stairs, following Quincy as he led her to Ellie, who was just coming out of the king's suite. She heard the king's final murmured words to her as she closed the door behind her.

"Here you go," Quincy said, then shuffled off to do whatever it was he did when he wasn't butlering—possibly getting himself a little nip of sherry.

"Amelia!" Eleanor said as she shoved some papers into her briefcase. "You didn't have to escort me down. I just wanted to pop in and say hi to everyone."

"But I wanted to speak to you privately," Amelia said. Not here in the hallway, though, where someone might overhear. She led Ellie into an empty suite across the hall from Easton's quarters and closed the door.

"Why all the mystery?"

"Is Nick still in New York?"

Ellie looked at her watch. "For about forty more minutes. His plane leaves at 2:05."

"Plane to where?"

"To Korosol, of course. Where did you think?"

"LaGuardia, or JFK?" Amelia asked urgently.

"JFK."

"What airline?"

"Air France, I think. Amelia, what is this about?"

She gave Ellie a quick hug. "I don't have time to explain. Tell the family I'm…running an errand."

She sprinted down the hall to her own room, not really thinking or planning her actions, just running on pure instinct. There was no time to order the limo—she would have to take a taxi. She'd regretted her decision to abandon Nick and the kids to the fates. This was the only way to make it right again.

From her room she grabbed big sunglasses, a hat and a long, bulky jacket that disguised her figure, which sometimes drew unintended attention despite the fact she did little to show it off. As she crept down the main stairs, she stuffed her telltale blond curls into the hat, shoved the glasses onto her face and donned the jacket.

She would have to sneak past the security station. The guard on duty couldn't keep his eyes on everything at the same time. While he checked the various monitors, she darted past him to the elevator. Ordinarily she was expected to let security know where she was going, but she didn't have time for lengthy explanations.

Her luck held—no one saw her exit the Carradignes' private elevator. Walking without her usual bold stride and confident gaze, shuffling along staring at the ground in front of her, she was a master at blending into crowds when she had to.

Once outside, she quickly secured a cab. "JFK,

please, and there's an extra twenty in it for you if you make it to the Air France gate in thirty minutes.''

"Yes, lady!" the Ethiopian driver said. He punched the gas pedal and the car jolted forward.

Amelia's luck held out as they encountered no traffic jams in the Queens Tunnel. The cabbie made it with two minutes to spare. Amelia shoved some cash at him and leaped out of the taxi without a backward glance.

She found the flight to Korosol on the Air France monitor. It was on time, probably the only flight all afternoon that wasn't running behind. So much for luck. She dashed through the airport until she reached the gate, which was devoid of passengers. Everyone had boarded already, but the plane was still at the gate.

Amelia zeroed in on the ticket agent. "I really need to speak to someone on that plane," she implored.

"I'm sorry, ma'am, but I can't— Oh my gosh, you're Princess Amelia."

Amelia decided that for once she could use her royal heritage to advantage. "Yes, I am, and this is a matter of great importance to…to the royal family." Well, a small part of it, anyway.

The ticket agent conferred with her co-worker, then looked back at Amelia. "The passenger's name?"

"Nicholas Standish."

She began punching buttons on her computer, driving Amelia wild with impatience. What was she doing?

The agent appeared confused. "Nicholas Standish is on the list, but he never checked onto this flight. Neither did Jakob or Josie Standish."

Amelia stifled a gasp. It was just as she feared.

Nick was running away with the kids. *Think, Mellie, think.* What would be his plan? He would go somewhere where he and the children could speak the language. Of course, Nick could speak half a dozen languages with some facility. But the children...only three. English, Russian and some French.

Canada—it had to be Canada. She thanked the agent, then walked as briskly as she dared without drawing attention down the terminal toward Canadian Airways.

He would go to a big city, where he could become anonymous. Quebec? Toronto? They spoke French in Quebec. Amelia checked the monitor. One flight had left at one-thirty, another was scheduled for three-fifteen. She went to the gate for the later flight. No Nick, no children.

Her hopes sank. Finding Nick in this airport would be like finding a particular grain of sand on a beach. He might have taken a completely different airline. For that matter, he might have gone to a different airport. Or he might be driving across the border with forged documents.

Amelia had one last idea. She went to an information phone and dialed the operator. "I need to page Nicholas Standish. Can you ask him to meet...his wife at the Canadian Airways ticket counter?"

"Yes, ma'am, I'd be happy to do that for you."

A few seconds later, the page went out over the loudspeaker. Amelia found a chair across from Canadian Airways and sat down to watch and wait.

NICK NEARLY JUMPED out of his skin when he heard his name over the loudspeaker.

"Uncle Nick, they just called your name," Josie

said, sounding alarmed. ''Are we in trouble for missing our plane?''

Nick smiled at her. ''No, Josie. But I'd better find out what's going on.'' The only person who knew he was here was Ellie. His hopes rose. Maybe she had news from the king. Maybe Easton had changed his mind.

He and the children had missed their flight to Korosol. They'd had plenty of time, but as he stood in line to check in, Nick hadn't been able to take that next step. He wasn't sure why. Clearly there was nothing else to be done to further his cause in New York. But the thought of returning to his village and waiting passively while the Ministry of Family took steps to remove his children…well, it was a difficult step to take.

He'd taken the kids to a fast-food place and bought them chocolate shakes to give him some time to think, though the previous two days of thinking hadn't yielded good results.

There was a courtesy phone right across from the restaurant where they'd gotten the shakes. Nick could answer the page and still keep watch over the kids.

''Be right back,'' he said. Moments later he was talking to an operator.

''Yes, Mr. Standish. Your wife would like you to meet her at the Canadian Airways ticket counter.''

''My wife?'' Not Ellie, then. Couldn't be anyone but Amelia. His heart beat double time at the implications her words conjured up. What was the princess up to this time? And how the hell had she figured out he was thinking about Canada? ''Thank you.''

Though he'd studiously avoided returning her calls, there was no way he could ignore Amelia's summons.

He gathered up the kids and luggage—thankfully they'd traveled light, having planned for only a weekend—and headed for the rendezvous point, walking so fast that Josie had to trot to keep up with him.

He saw Amelia before she saw him. Though she'd hidden her magnificent gold hair under a hat and wore huge dark glasses, he was intimately familiar with her body language. She sat in a chair with one knee drawn up under the skirt of her flowery dress. He tried to summon some anger against her for the torture she'd caused him, but right now she looked so worried he realized she carried some burdens of her own.

"Auntie Mellie!" Jakob squirmed from Nick's arms and ran toward Amelia, whose face lit up with joy at the sight of him—at all of them. She rose and welcomed Jakob into a hug. Whether the boy remembered Amelia from Palemeir, he'd certainly taken a shine to her here in New York.

"What's she doing here?" Josie asked, instantly suspicious.

"I don't know. But I'm going to find out."

Amelia had a smile for Josie, too, but when she looked up at Nick, the smile faded and she looked almost…afraid. "Oh my God, I can't believe I found you. I was taking a stab in the dark with that page, but you weren't on the Air France flight to Korosol, and I was so worried you'd run off to Canada or someplace—I'm babbling, aren't I?"

Nick nodded. Yes, he'd thought about fleeing. He'd even talked to an expert document forger about false passports and birth certificates for him and the kids. But that would be a last resort. Becoming a fugitive would mean no more contact with Eleanor, and that would be tough—not to mention what it might do to the kids.

"Is there a problem?" Nick asked. "Something wrong with my sister?"

"No, nothing like that. You missed your plane. Why?"

He shrugged. "I don't know. I guess I was hoping I'd come up with a plan for changing King Easton's mind, but…"

"We don't have to change his mind," Amelia said with quiet determination. "I've got a plan of my own. Now, it might not be ideal, but I believe it will get the social workers off your back."

"Okay, I'm listening."

Amelia suddenly clammed up, looking uneasy.

"What plan?" Josie prompted, proving she'd been paying close attention to the conversation.

"This is a little awkward," Amelia said, glancing at first one child, then the other. "Maybe you and I should discuss it in private first."

Josie rolled her eyes. "C'mon, Jakob, they're going to talk about grown-up things." She took her little brother's hand and led him to the far end of the row of chairs, taking her brightly colored rolling suitcase with her. As soon as Nick was sure the children were safely absorbed with a toy, he turned his attention back to Amelia, his curiosity overflowing.

"Just tell me."

"Okay." She took a deep breath. "Well, see, if the Ministry of Family objects to the fact our marriage was a sham, we need to prove to them it wasn't. We'll tell them we intended to make it real, but my family objected and ordered me back home—"

"I tried that already."

"I'm not finished. Words obviously won't convince them. Only actions. I'm suggesting, Nick, that we get married again—nice and legal this time."

Chapter Four

Nick was so stunned he could say nothing at all for a few moments. Then, his first instinct was to say, *No way.* Marrying Amelia was what had gotten him into this jam in the first place.

But everything she'd said was true. He had told the Ministry of Family the exact story she'd just related—that they'd fallen in love and intended to be a family, but the royal family had intervened and forced them to separate.

"Nick? You're not saying anything."

"Give me a minute. You've surprised me, to say the least."

"I surprised myself. But I cannot allow those precious children to be taken from you, not after everything they've been through."

Nick finally began to recover from the shock and think rationally about Amelia's suggestion. It was crazy—him marrying a princess—but it just might work. It would certainly lend credence to the story he'd told the government officials. He turned the idea over in his head a few times, trying to find its flaws.

One, in particular, came up immediately. "If your

family tore us apart before, why would they now let you marry me?"

"It's not like I need their permission," she huffed. "This is an enlightened age. I can marry whom I want. I let them interfere a year ago because I was scared and confused. But seeing you and the children again made me realize we should all be together. You've realized it, too—that's why you came."

She sounded so sincere, *he* almost believed her. "Are you bucking for an Academy Award?"

"I only want to convince you it will work."

"And what will the terms of this marriage be?" He wanted to know.

"We'll have a simple ceremony, family only."

He was less concerned with the details of the wedding itself than the events afterward. "You'll come back with us to Korosol?"

"I haven't thought that far ahead. I was thinking the wedding itself would be enough to do the trick."

"Will we stay married?" he asked quietly.

"Long enough to be convincing. Then we can quietly separate."

"Long enough? A few days? Weeks? What? And you actually think a princess can 'quietly separate'?"

He'd caught her there. Her gaze slid away from his. "I haven't worked out all the details yet. But it'll work, I know it will."

Nick took a deep breath. This was about the most bloodless proposal he'd ever—then again, when the tables had been turned and he'd been proposing marriage to "Melanie," he'd been just as pragmatic, just as emotionless. He'd wanted her name on a marriage license so he could get those kids out of Palemeir, and he'd given her no other reason.

Maybe if, at that time, he'd confessed his physical desire for her, his genuine affection and respect for her, things would have turned out differently. Certainly he didn't like the idea that he'd made Amelia feel then as he felt now—forced to say yes for the children's sake.

"I assume you would want a prenuptial agreement. You keep your money, I keep the kids."

She hesitated. "If that's what you want." She paused, then looked at him quizzically. "Does this mean you'll do it?"

"Do I have a choice?"

"Well, you don't have to make it sound like I've proposed tar and feathering."

"Forgive me if I don't jump up and down. I realize you're making a sacrifice on behalf of the children, and I appreciate it. But I resent the government pushing me around, forcing us to go to these ridiculous lengths just so I can keep two children who any idiot can see belong with me."

"It's not really such a sacrifice," she said quietly. "I want to help. And I was, after all, the one who contributed to the dilemma in the first place."

"Have you mentioned your little plan to your family?"

"Actually, it was my sister Lucia who thought of it."

"Not the sister I met."

"No, that was CeCe. Lucia's the youngest. Very creative."

"So your family approves of this decision?"

She hesitated again. "Not exactly. I haven't mentioned it to my mother, and certainly not to the king."

She looked distinctly uneasy at that proposition. "They'll just have to accept it."

"Then I guess we're engaged." He took Amelia's hand and led her over to the children. It was amazing how delicate her hand felt in his, like the bones might break if he weren't careful. But he knew that impression was deceiving. Her hands were strong and capable, but gentle, too. He'd often wondered how they would feel on his body.

He didn't imagine he would get to find out. Amelia was marrying him for the sake of his children, not to satisfy his libidinous curiosity.

Josie and Jakob looked up from their play. "Children, your uncle Nick is going to marry a princess."

"Does this mean we'll get to stay with you?" Josie asked, hope lighting her eyes for the first time since she arrived in New York. He was amazed how sharp her mind was, how quickly she figured things out.

"Yes, it does," Nick said.

"Auntie Mellie will live with us?" Jakob asked. "She'll be our mama?"

Amelia gave a small gasp. She started to say something, but Josie beat her to it.

"No," Josie said sharply. "Our mother is dead."

Jakob's little face fell.

Nick felt an alien urge to pick up the child and cuddle him. But while protecting these children came as second nature, showing them love or affection was another matter entirely. He knew they needed love, but he wasn't the one who could give it to them.

"Your real mother is in heaven, Jakob," he finally said. "And you'll always love her in a special way because she brought you into the world."

"But can Auntie Mellie be Mama, too?"

Amelia looked at Nick, her eyes pleading with him not to blow this. Hell, he didn't have the slightest idea what to say.

"She's Auntie Mellie," Josie said stubbornly. "Don't be a baby, Jakob."

"I'm happy just being your auntie," Amelia said, finding her voice. She pulled her hand from Nick's light grasp and crouched down until she was at Jakob's level. "We'll take this one day at a time, okay? We don't know yet who is going to live where and when. But we do know that you kids will stay with your uncle Nick, no matter what. Okay?"

Both children nodded, but Nick was feeling a bit shell-shocked from the conversation. Jakob had never once expressed any interest in calling Nick "Papa."

AMELIA'S HEART hadn't stopped pounding since Nick had agreed to marry her. She must be out of her mind, to make such a sudden decision without consulting anyone, and carry it out so quickly.

She was committed now, though. She'd waffled with Nick once before, and she intended to keep her word this time. But the real test was whether they could actually make the marriage happen. Her grandfather was not going to be happy with her choice of husband, and she feared what actions he might take against Nick, who was a Korosolian and subject to Easton's rule. What if the king had Nick arrested? Easton said he didn't like interfering in private citizens' affairs, but he might change his mind in a hurry when it came to a threat to the royal succession.

As they rode up the private elevator to the Carradigne penthouse, Amelia's apprehension grew. She'd spouted a lot of brave words to Nick about how she was a modern woman free to marry whom she chose, but when it came right down to it, she was afraid of displeasing her mother. Though Amelia got along better with Charlotte than her two sisters did, Charlotte had always been faintly disapproving of her middle daughter's obsession with war orphans and her lack of interest in matters closer to home.

Amelia doubted Charlotte would jump for joy over her daughter marrying an ex-mercenary. She had certainly *not* taken the news of Amelia and Nick's first "marriage" well.

The elevator opened onto the foyer. Amelia gave a nod and a smile to Quincy, who'd been dozing at his post. He looked surprised to see her.

"Where did you come from?" Quincy asked.

"Oh, just out," she said breezily. "Could you be a dear, Quincy, and round up the family? I have an important announcement to make. Ask them to meet in the Grand Room."

Quincy stood up and nodded. "Yes, Miss Amelia, right away." He scurried off to do her bidding.

She turned back to her soon-to-be family. "Big news like this deserves a formal setting." She led Nick and the children into the huge formal living area that was used for entertaining.

"How many rooms does this house have?" Josie asked.

"More than any one family needs," Amelia replied, thinking about the two-room apartment the children had occupied in Palemeir. And that home had been considered luxurious accommodations. Sometimes Amelia felt guilty over the opulence of her lifestyle in America when she was faced with how the less fortunate lived.

"But I bet it's not as fancy as the royal palace," Josie said. "Back home, I mean."

"No, it's not." She scooped up Jakob just before he could grab a Waterford vase to inspect it more closely. "I haven't been since I was a little girl, so I don't remember much, but I do remember that the king has a bathroom bigger than this room, all done in pink marble, and it has a gold bathtub."

Josie's eyes lit up. "Is your father a king?" she asked, obviously trying to work out Amelia's place in the royal family.

"No, he was a prince, but he was never in line for the throne. He married an American—my mother— and they decided to live here." She wanted to talk longer with Josie. It wasn't often the girl dropped her guard around Amelia. But just then her mother entered, followed by CeCe and Shane, Lucia, Hester and Quincy.

Amelia was relieved to see that the king wasn't with them. He would have to be told, but she'd prefer to deal with him later rather than sooner.

"Amelia, what is this all about?" Charlotte asked worriedly. CeCe, Lucia and Hester just smiled when they saw Nick and the children. They already suspected what was going on.

"Mother," Amelia said, "I'd like you to meet Nicholas Standish, and his children, Josie and Jakob."

"*Adopted* children," Josie clarified haughtily. She was not going to let anyone slight her birth parents.

Charlotte's smile was guarded. She took Nick's proffered hand and gave it a perfunctory shake. "I've heard a lot about you, Mr. Standish."

"I might say the same."

The tightly controlled lines of her face softened as she looked on the children. "How very charming. Oh, it's been so long since we had little ones around here."

"I'm big," Jakob objected.

"Of course," Charlotte said. "A very big boy indeed."

Amelia introduced Nick to those he hadn't already met, and an awkward silence descended on them as everyone found a place to sit.

"Should I have Bernice bring us some refreshment?" Hester asked.

"That's an excellent idea," Amelia said. "See if she can scrounge up some champagne."

"Champagne?" Charlotte repeated, sounding alarmed.

Amelia was about to blurt out the news when Nick gave her a look that squelched the words. He then proceeded to shock her to her core by standing and doing the deed himself.

"Lady Charlotte, Princess Cecelia, Princess Lucia and other assembled family and friends..." He paused dramatically. "Princess Amelia has graciously agreed to be my wife—legally this time."

CeCe and Shane shared a look of pleasure. And Charlotte's mouth dropped in an unladylike gape. Hester fanned herself as if about to swoon. Lucia gave a knowing smirk.

Amelia herself probably looked shocked over Nick's courtly announcement, but she recovered as quickly as possible. She knew what Nick was doing. He'd realized that the fewer people who knew the true reasons for their marriage, the better—especially given the unknown spy who was providing gossip to Krissy Katwell.

After a few moments of stunned silence, Charlotte composed herself and addressed Amelia.

"Amelia, is this true?"

"Yes, Mother, of course it's true." Nick gave her a look, which she interpreted to mean he wanted her to play along, and she obliged. "We shared a lot in Palemeir, and although we married the first time to expedite Josie and Jakob's adoption, we had also grown quite...fond of each other."

"And when I saw Amelia again," Nick said, taking up the story, "I realized I couldn't let her go a second time."

"This *does* call for champagne," Hester said, beaming as she scurried out of the room. Quincy followed her, probably off to share the gossip with the rest of the staff before they heard it from someone else—or have a quick nip of the champagne himself.

"Amelia," Charlotte said, "have you thought this through? And Mr. Standish, please understand, my reservations have nothing to do with you personally. It's just that as a member of Korosol's royal family, Amelia must—"

"I've thought it through," Amelia said, which was not exactly true. She was being her usual impulsive self. But she knew to what Charlotte referred. The king was going to blow a gasket. "I'd like to be sensitive to my...obligations, but I also have to do what's right for me."

"Mother," Lucia said, "surely you understand marrying for love. If Father had worried about 'royal obligations,' he never would have married you."

Charlotte frowned harder. "Thank you, Lucia, for that lovely reminder."

"Well, I, for one, am going to offer my congratulations." Lucia came forward and hugged an unprepared Nick. "Nicholas, congratulations on your engagement. Amelia, best wishes." She hugged Amelia, too.

Once Lucia broke the ice, the others got into the act, offering congratulations and hugs. When the champagne arrived, along with juice for the children, the occasion turned downright festive.

Charlotte, however, refused to soften. "I don't suppose I can talk you out of this?" she said to Amelia. "You could at least talk to Easton first and try to gain his approval."

"I'll talk to him. But we're going ahead with the marriage, with or without his blessing."

"As soon as possible," Nick added, playing the part of the eager bridegroom.

Charlotte sighed. "Then I suppose this means we get to plan another wedding. The king is more likely to support this marriage if we present a united front."

Nick caught Jakob just before the child barreled into a table that held a collection of priceless porcelain figurines. "Jakob, try to be careful, okay? We don't want to break anything."

"Okay, Uncle Nick," Jakob said earnestly, just before his juice glass slipped out of his hand and spilled all over the Oriental rug.

"I'll get that, don't you worry," Hester said.

"We'll need at least two months to make the plans," Charlotte said, unable to stop herself from moving into full strategic planning mode. "That will put us into—oh dear, things start getting dicey in May. We can forget reserving the church, but—''

''Mother, I really don't want a big wedding. CeCe's was so beautiful, and with it so fresh on everyone's mind, the comparisons will be inevitable. I'd like to have a small ceremony, family only.''

''And, much as we're enjoying New York,'' Nick said, ''I can't stay here indefinitely. I need to get Josie back in school.''

''I don't need to go to school,'' Josie said hopefully.

Charlotte looked troubled. ''Amelia, dear, does this mean—are you going to live in Korosol?''

''We haven't made a decision about where we'll live,'' Amelia said breezily. ''Since I'm an American citizen, if Nick marries me he can relocate here if he likes, but he tells me his village in Korosol is lovely.''

Nick gave her a look that said, *Take it easy with the playacting.* He was right, she knew. The less said, the less likely she and Nick would be caught in a deception. But, to her surprise, she found it extraordinarily easy to pretend to be the giddy bride about to marry the man of her dreams.

Extraordinarily easy.

They decided on the following Friday for the wedding. Charlotte declared she couldn't possibly make the arrangements by then, even for a small ceremony, but Amelia held firm. She chose to have the ceremony on the terrace, weather permitting, and the reception here in the Grand Room.

''You haven't said much,'' Charlotte said to Nick. ''Do these plans suit you?''

''Whatever Amelia wants is fine with me,'' he said

with a beatific smile. Amelia found herself wishing Nick wasn't such a good actor.

Later, Lucia took Amelia aside, looking far too serious for a woman who'd downed at least two glasses of champagne. "I can't believe you actually listened to me for a change," she whispered. "I didn't think in a million years you would do this."

"I didn't either," Amelia said. "But the more I thought about it, the more I realized it was the right thing to do."

"But what is Grandfather going to do when he finds out?"

"That's what worries me."

"When are you going to tell him?"

"Not until I have to."

"He's going to fire you as queen-elect, you know."

"I know." Unexpectedly, her throat felt thick. She hadn't realized that any part of her truly wanted to be queen. She might be throwing away an opportunity most people only dreamed of. Still, she owed it to the children to ensure they got to stay with Nick.

"What if he comes to me next?" Lucia asked, for the first time seriously considering the possibility. "I know we joke about it, but it's possible. He seems kind of...fond of me."

Amelia acknowledged this was true. Lucia seemed to amuse the king. He was stiff and formal with everyone but her, and he even allowed her to tease him a bit. "Would it be so bad, being queen?" Amelia asked. "Just think of the reforms you could enact. Free rock concerts at the palace every weekend. And what a boost it would give your jewelry business."

"Ha ha, very funny. Well, no use worrying about something that probably won't happen. I just hope you know what you're doing with Nick. I know it was my idea to begin with, but...you two aren't really in love, are you?''

Amelia didn't quite know how to answer that one. She did have feelings for the man. He might be cool and reserved now, but deep down she knew Nick Standish had a deep well of feelings. "He's a good actor," she finally said. "We're planning to divorce the moment the children are secure."

Lucia looked sad after this pronouncement, but she didn't argue.

Charlotte invited Nick and the children to stay at the penthouse for the time being, but he declined. Amelia had mixed feelings about that. It would be easier to get through the week without the added tension his presence brought. On the other hand, she craved his nearness. There definitely was *something* simmering between them.

"We don't want to get in the way while you are concentrating on the wedding plans," Nick said easily. More likely, Amelia thought, he just didn't want to spend that much time with the royal family, or with her. He seemed ever so slightly derisive about the whole idea of royalty, and she wouldn't blame him if his resentments ran deep, especially after King Easton's refusal to help him keep the children.

She also hadn't forgotten what Ellie had told her about Nick's past. He might feel guilty over remarrying, especially in such spectacular fashion. Unlike their first quickie wedding, this time the world would be watching, no matter how hard they tried to keep the press out of it.

After Nick and the children returned to their hotel, Charlotte took Amelia aside.

"Are you sure you know what you're doing?"

"Yes, Mother." *No, not in the least.*

"This just seems so crazy. I don't know what Easton's going to do when he finds out."

"What *can* he do? He's on American soil, he can't stop the wedding."

"Yes, but he could take the crown away from you. Think about it—you're turning your back on the opportunity to rule a country. The world needs sensible, intelligent rulers like you—even if you aren't being so sensible now."

"I'm perfectly willing to do it, if he still wants me," Amelia said. "But if the king wants to choose another successor because I want to help two children, then so be it."

Chapter Five

"What's our next stop?" Nick asked as he and Amelia rode down the elevator in the mirrored skyscraper that housed the law firm used by the Carradignes.

Amelia checked her schedule. One day after announcing their engagement, they'd already applied for the license and had a blood test. They'd visited the lawyer to sign the hastily written prenup. "Counseling," she declared.

"You're kidding, right?"

"Reverend Baker was willing to marry us quickly, but he insists we come in for at least one premarital-counseling session. I, um, told him we'd drop by this afternoon."

"Oh, great. I haven't been to church in years."

"You don't take the children to church?"

"No," he admitted. "We talk a lot about right and wrong, but organized religion isn't my forte."

Amelia touched his arm. "That's okay. Reverend Baker is pretty cool, and his grandparents were from Korosol. He won't be too tough on us."

"What will we talk about?" Nick wanted to know.

It seemed amusing to Amelia that Nick was so apprehensive about a minister. Without blinking he'd faced bands of guerrillas and rioting civilians with guns, but this, apparently, was uncharted territory.

"I'm not sure what goes on in premarital counseling—I've never gotten married before—except to you. But it can't be that bad."

NICK WASN'T SO SURE about that. He'd seen some of the horror enacted in the name of religion, so he was less than enthusiastic about organized churchgoing. Still, children did need some spiritual guidance. Perhaps when he was home he'd look into attending church again, and just make sure he and the kids kept an open dialogue about things sacred.

The Carradigne limo whisked them through the streets of Manhattan to an imposing granite church. The faint smell of incense and candle wax brought back childhood memories.

Reverend Baker, a slight, nervous man of indeterminate age, met them in the sacristy and led them to a small sitting room furnished with several comfortable-looking chairs and one love seat. Reverend Baker nodded toward the love seat, indicating they should sit.

"Marriage is certainly in the air with the Carradigne princesses," he remarked jovially. "Cecelia marrying her business partner was surprising. But your sudden betrothal—well, it's more of a shock, especially after the, er, publicity."

The Carradignes' PR agency had categorically denied Krissy Katwell's allegations that Princess Amelia was married to Nicholas Standish, so Nick supposed this latest turn of events would be confusing to the public as well as the priest. Not that he cared a whit what the public thought.

"I know it seems sudden," Amelia said, "but Nick and I met almost a year ago. We've both decided marriage is the right thing to do."

Nick reached over and took her hand in his. She jumped, then relaxed. They'd touched each other very little since he'd come to New York, but they would have to get used to looking like a real couple if they wanted to convince anyone theirs was a real marriage.

"Is there any particular reason for the rush to the altar?" Reverend Baker asked. "Or is it just impatience to be living as husband and wife?"

"There was no reason to wait," Nick said. "We don't want a big, extravagant wedding."

"Very well, then," Reverend Baker said with a smile. "Are you of the same faith?"

Amelia looked at Nick. Nick nodded. "I confess I haven't been the most ardent churchgoer, but I intend to mend my ways, especially because I—we have two children to raise."

Reverend Baker nodded his approval. "Then you'll be raising the children in the faith as well. Excellent. We won't have to argue about that." He laughed at his own little joke. "Where will you live?"

Again, Amelia looked at Nick. He didn't know how to answer that one. Finally she came up with a response. "We don't know for sure yet. For the immediate future, we'll be staying at my mother's. But Nick has a home in Korosol, and other property. I guess the short answer is, we'll be dividing our time between Korosol and America."

That answer didn't seem to please the minister. "You don't think that will be too disruptive for the children?"

"I would never do anything detrimental to the children, believe me," Nick said. "I didn't save their lives only to harm them later. I believe a certain amount of travel is good for children—exposing them to new cultures, meeting new people. But stability is important, too, and it's not something I'm likely to overlook. I'm sure we'll spend time in the town where I've retired to, Montavi. It's quiet there."

This whole discussion was moot, anyway. Once the Ministry of Family was off his back, there would be no need to travel to America. Amelia and the whole royal clan would be out of their lives.

Nick seemed to have pleased Reverend Baker, because he moved on to other things.

"You've both led somewhat…adventurous lives," the priest said. "Do you plan to continue flying into third world countries and such?"

Amelia tensed. Her humanitarian efforts were a touchy subject with her right now. King Easton had forbidden her to continue what he considered to be dangerous activities. Though she was not subject to his rule, he was her grandfather, and out of respect for him she had agreed. But it obviously wasn't sitting well with her.

"The answer to that isn't simple," she said. "For now, at least, I'm not planning to participate in any relief efforts. A married woman has to make some compromises."

The minister turned to Nick. "And you, Nicholas?"

"I'm officially retired. The most dangerous thing I face in my village is an occasional stray sheep darting across the road in front of my bicycle."

Again seeming satisfied, Reverend Baker talked about ways to deal with conflicts, the need for each of them to cultivate outside interests, how to share household responsibilities and child-rearing.

He had to squelch laughter at some of the points the minister made. Amelia probably never touched a dish or a mop at the penthouse. She had a bevy of servants to do those mundane chores. But then he remembered how hard she'd worked at the Palemeir refugee camp to cook beans and rice for the children, organizing meals with the efficiency of a general, making sure no child went hungry even if she did— and washing the dishes afterward.

She was no pampered poodle, no stranger to hard work. That was one of the many things he'd admired about "Melanie Lacey," before he'd known she was a princess.

"And have you discussed having more children?" Reverend Baker asked, jolting Nick from his reverie. "I know you'll have your hands full with two war orphans, but the Lord may soon bless you with more babies."

Amelia looked like a cat startled by the vacuum cleaner. He considered coming to her rescue, but he was curious how she would answer.

Finally she did, and her sentiments surprised him. "Of course, I would welcome more children," she said, sounding completely sincere. "All my life, I've wanted children of my own. My peculiar circumstances have made normal dating relationships almost impossible, and I despaired of ever meeting someone I could have a family with. I even thought about adopting orphans on my own. Now I've been lucky enough to find a family starter package. And as far as I'm concerned, the more the merrier."

Reverend Baker beamed. "I take it you concur, Nick?"

Suddenly Nick couldn't find any words, so he just nodded. He could have sworn Amelia wasn't acting just now. She *did* cherish Josie and Jakob. He'd thought it strange a princess would marry someone like him out of kindness alone. Now he realized there was something in this for Amelia as well. She would get the family she'd always dreamed of—at least, temporarily.

How would she handle it when he and the kids removed themselves from her life for good, as they inevitably would?

"WHEN ARE YOU GOING to talk to Easton?" Charlotte asked Amelia point-blank the next day. They were in the Grand Room, watching as a trio of models paraded before them one at a time, each one wearing a wedding dress more ghastly than the last.

"Can't we just wait until Friday?"

"Amelia, dear, you know his reaction will only be worse if you aren't forthright with him. If he reads the news in some gossip column—"

"Heaven forbid! All right, I'll talk to him as soon as he gets back from the embassy today." She lowered her voice. "My Lord, what is that?" Her comment was directed toward a voluminous cloud of chiffon with a hoop skirt, a scalloped hemline and a bodice festooned with pink satin roses.

"I think it's beautiful," Charlotte said. "Just the thing for a princess."

Amelia suspected Charlotte's praise was for the sake of the designer, Yuki Yamazaki. Amelia had resisted going to Yuki's shop, declaring she would just buy a dress off the rack, quickly and inexpensively. But Yuki had insisted on staging this impromptu fashion show in hopes of getting the contract for yet another royal wedding gown. She'd done CeCe's, which had been gorgeous.

"It looks beautiful on the model," Amelia agreed. "But I'm a bit…curvier. I'm afraid the dress would make me look like the Sta-Puff Marshmallow Man."

Charlotte nudged her in the ribs.

"Well, I'm just trying to be honest," Amelia said. "I look better in a dress with simple lines." *Like maybe one that was already in her closet.*

The first time she'd married Nick, she'd been wearing camouflage fatigues. All this formality seemed ridiculous.

"I don't have anything simple with me," Yuki said glumly.

"But you could create something before Friday, couldn't you?" Charlotte asked.

Yuki immediately brightened. "Of course I can. And I know just the thing," the Japanese woman said, dismissing the models with a clap of her hands. She opened her briefcase, pulled out a pad and pencil and quickly sketched something, then showed it to Amelia, with Charlotte peering over her shoulder. "Off-white raw silk flowing from the bustline to the floor. Short sleeved, like this, but with a plain satin wrap around the shoulders. And gloves, you must have gloves. With your natural curves enhanced, Princess Amelia, you will look like a goddess."

Amelia's interest was piqued despite her fatigue. "Yes, that's just what I want. No lace, no seed pearls, no rickrack, no scallops, no satin roses—"

"Yes, Amelia, I'm sure Yuki gets the idea."

"We'll have a fitting on Thursday, if that meets with your approval, Your Highness."

Amelia gritted her teeth at the formal address. She despised all this froufrou stuff. She wanted to be jogging on a beach somewhere, alone. Or maybe with Nick. She didn't mind his company, even when he was frowning and noncommunicative. They had chemistry, if nothing else.

As soon as Yuki and her bevy of models had left, Amelia tried to escape to her room for a much-needed rest, but Charlotte prevented her flight. "We need to make a decision about the flowers."

Amelia didn't really care, but she knew that to say so would upset her mother. "Something easy. How about daisies? I like the way they can grow anywhere. They push up in the cracks of a sidewalk, even in a war zone."

Charlotte looked horrified. "We'll go with roses. And those little purple flowers."

Their discussion was halted by the sound of the private-elevator bell ringing from the foyer. Amelia experienced a moment of panic. "Is that him?"

"I don't know who else it would be."

"I thought he wouldn't be here until dinner. They can't be done with the Bronx Zoo already."

Charlotte tittered with laughter. "Oh, my dear, I wasn't talking about Nicholas. I believe your dear grandfather is home. What I don't understand is why your own fiancé makes you so nervous."

"I'm...I'm still trying to impress him, I guess," Amelia said lamely. "This isn't my best outfit."

"Well, you've got more important things to worry about than impressing Nicholas. That is definitely the king. I'm learning to know his footsteps. And you'd better go to him—now.''

"I'd like to wait until Nick gets here tonight. You haven't forgotten he and the children are having dinner with us? We'll tell him together."

"Of course I haven't forgotten. And you're procrastinating. Do it now, or I will."

"Would you?" Amelia would do just about anything to weasel out of facing the king. She'd once faced down an army deserter with a gun who'd invaded her refugee camp trying to find food. He hadn't scared her nearly as much as the idea of the king's wrath. He was a formidable man.

EASTON WAS TIRED, and it infuriated him. He had the same keen mind he'd always had, always thinking, always moving, clicking on to the next item on his agenda. But his body didn't want to cooperate. It just wanted to take a nap.

He smelled a delightful scent wafting from the kitchen, and his stomach rumbled. He shouldn't have skipped lunch today. A man his age shouldn't make demands like that on a failing body, particularly when he had a rare blood disease that was slowly killing him. Now he wanted nothing more than to have Bernice prepare him a light meal and deliver it to his room, where he intended to eat and then indulge in that nap.

He started for the stairs, then paused. That scent— he could swear it was raspberry tarts, a favorite treat from childhood. Such rich foods were off his diet now. But he could at least enjoy the scent.

Easton headed into the kitchen, where Bernice was

rolling out pastry. She looked up, surprised to see him. "Your Majesty! Can I get you something?"

"Would you mind preparing a tray for me and delivering it to my room? Something light. And—what are you baking?"

"It was going to be a surprise for you. Miss Eleanor said raspberry tarts were one of your favorites, and she even gave me the palace chef's own recipe."

"Very thoughtful of her, and you."

"Would sliced turkey be all right?"

"Yes, that sounds delightful. I'll just go up to my—"

Amelia burst into the kitchen in her customary, less-than-dignified way. "Bernice, have you seen— oh, Grandfather, there you are."

"Just visiting with this delightful lady," Easton said, forcing a smile. The cook turned bright red and busied herself removing a sheet of tarts from the oven. The smell made Easton's mouth water.

"I need to speak to you," Amelia said.

"Could it wait? I'm really rather fatigued from—"

"It's important."

Easton couldn't imagine what disaster had befallen the Carradignes now. They seemed to be living a soap opera. At least the family's PR agency had taken care of that nonsense about Amelia being secretly married to a mercenary.

"Very well, my dear. Come with me up to my quarters, where we can relax."

"Oh, Amelia," Bernice said, "before you leave, your mother wants you to approve the menu for the wedding brunch."

"The *what?*" Easton roared.

Amelia turned white. "Um, I'll look at it later, Bernice." She hastily took Easton's arm and hustled him out of the kitchen.

"What wedding?" Easton demanded as they climbed the back stairs. "What have you done *now?*"

"Please don't be upset," Amelia said. "I can explain everything."

"Who's getting married? It's not Lucia and that dreadful rock singer, is it?"

Amelia sighed as they entered Easton's suite. "It's me."

"Exactly whom do you think you're marrying?"

"Nick. Nicholas Standish. Your secretary's brother."

"The one you married unlawfully in Palemeir. Amelia, I thought that scandal was all behind you."

"I thought it was, too. But you see, Nick and I really do care for each other, and—"

"It's impossible." Easton sat down in a satin-covered wingback chair. "You cannot marry without my approval. There are dynastic considerations. Korosol won't accept your marrying a commoner."

"What about CeCe? Shane doesn't have a title."

"Your sister was carrying Shane's child. Anyway, Shane is a wealthy, respected businessman. Nicholas Standish is a common soldier of fortune—even if he is retired. That simply isn't suitable. It just isn't done. Forget it."

"Begging Your Majesty's indulgence," Amelia said in a formal tone he'd never heard before. She usually was refreshingly casual. "These are modern times, and no one—queen or peasant—should marry for reasons other than love and commitment. Look at what happens when people don't. There are plenty of tragic royal liaisons in the history books."

"I'm not saying you can't love the man you marry. You'll have your choice of dozens of titled gentlemen, any one of whom you can fall in love with. But as a future queen, you have responsibilities, and sometimes you must make sacrifices. We've discussed this before."

"Your Majesty, may I speak in confidence?"

"Of course you can speak in confidence. You think I'm going to run off and jabber to that dreadful columnist?"

"If I don't marry Nick, he might very well lose those adorable children. I'll make personal sacrifices, but I won't sacrifice children. This marriage is for them."

"I forbid it. There must be dozens of women who would marry Nicholas and be a mother to the children."

"The Ministry of Family won't accept a quickie marriage-of-convenience. But they'll accept me because Nick and I have a history. A true marriage between us is believable."

"Nevertheless, I forbid it."

"Then talk to the Ministry of Family. Get them to leave Nick alone, and the wedding won't be necessary."

"Dear God, are you blackmailing the king?" Easton couldn't believe his ears, though he wasn't as horrified as he pretended. He wanted to see that crown on her head before he left this world. But first he had to disabuse her of this notion that she could up and marry an ex-mercenary. He'd already gotten a taste of the scandal it would create. Quite impossible.

"I'm merely making my position clear. Your Majesty."

Cheeky girl. "There will be no wedding."

"Yes, there will be. This Friday evening, on the terrace, family and close friends only. With or without your blessing. I am an American citizen on American soil."

"You realize you're jeopardizing the royal succession."

"Yes, I do."

"You also realize you've displeased me greatly. I've invested a lot of time and faith in you."

"I know. And I apologize. But I have to do what's right in my heart."

Easton gave his spunky granddaughter his worst scowl. "Leave me now."

"Yes, Your Majesty." Amelia actually curtsied and backed out of the room.

The moment he was alone, he got on the telephone and contacted Harrison Montcalm, his most senior adviser. "Harrison? I have a job for you. I want every piece of information you can dig up about Nicholas Standish."

"The one who was supposedly married to Princess Amelia?"

"That's the one."

"Isn't he your secretary's brother?"

"Yes, he is. However, I don't want Eleanor to know I'm looking into his background. Can you be discreet?"

"Yes, Your Majesty."

Easton hung up the phone, knowing he could count on Harrison to do the job and do it right.

Chapter Six

Amelia could feel the perspiration dripping inside her clothes as she made her escape to her own room. That had gone even worse than she'd imagined. Her grandfather was *furious*.

She looked longingly at her bed. Oh, how she wanted a nap. But it was late afternoon, and if she lay down now, she would ruin her sleep tonight. Never had she suffered from insomnia until this week. If this was bridal jitters, she was glad she wouldn't have to put up with them for long. Long engagements were for the birds.

The sound of children chattering distracted her from her thoughts of sleep. Josie and Jakob were here, and that meant their father was, too. She had to tell him about her encounter with His Majesty—before the two men ran into each other in the hallway and Nick found himself with a broken nose.

Amelia headed into the foyer, just managing to catch her quarry entering the Grand Room.

"Auntie Mellie!" Jakob barreled toward her. She caught him just as he would have knocked her over and swung him into his arms.

"Oof, Jakob, you're getting too big for this. Did you have fun at the zoo?"

"Yes, we saw an alligator and a seal!"

"We saw a lot more animals than that, Jakob," Josie said with authority.

"And what animals did you like, Josie?" Amelia asked.

"I liked them all, but I wish they didn't have to live behind fences. When I get to be a princess, I'll buy the zoo and let all the animals go."

"I would think the citizens of the Bronx might have something to say about that," Nick said, taking a squirming Jakob from Amelia's arms. "Come on, you two, I've got to get you cleaned up before dinner, or Lady Charlotte won't have you at her table. Is there a bathroom we can use?"

"I'll take the moppets upstairs for a quick shine," said Hester, who'd just entered to greet their guests.

"I could use a quick shine, too," Nick confessed. "We spent some time in the petting zoo. I smell like a goat."

He smelled like nothing except a very sexy man. Amelia resisted the urge to step closer to him and get a good noseful of his male essence.

"Let the kids go with Hester first," Amelia said. "I need a private word with you, Nick."

He looked a bit uncomfortable at the idea of being alone with her. In fact, he never let those kids get more than shouting distance away from him. As the children accompanied Hester out of the Grand Room, Nick's gaze followed them, as if gauging his chances of a clean escape. Apparently he decided he might as well face her now rather than later.

"Is there a problem?" he asked, wandering to the French doors that led out to the terrace.

"I talked to the king today. I told him about us."

Nick tensed. "How'd he take it?"

"Not very well, I'm afraid."

"I don't see why he should care. It's not like you're in line for the throne or anything."

Amelia felt every cell in her body jump in surprise. She wished she could tell Nick the truth about being selected as Korosol's future monarch. But only the king himself could release that information. Should news get out that the king was searching for his replacement, it could throw Korosol into turmoil.

"Is something wrong?" Nick asked.

"No. I just wanted to warn you. I don't think Grandfather will try to stop the wedding, but I wouldn't be surprised if he confronted you and tried to talk you out of it."

"Let him try. This wouldn't be necessary if he'd helped me in the first place."

"I pointed that out to him," she said. "He wasn't appreciative."

"Can he do anything to stop us? Legally, I mean."

"I don't think so. But I wouldn't put it past him to have you kidnapped or deported or something. He could go through diplomatic channels and have your visa revoked."

Nick turned to face her. "I thought he didn't like to throw his weight around."

"That's what he says." But when it came to what he perceived to be the good of the country, all bets were off.

"It would have been easier if we'd eloped."

"Maybe we still can," she said.

"That would just make everyone angry with us. Besides, a wedding implies family approval, which is just the sort of thing the Ministry of Family will look at."

Ah, yes, the omnipresent Ministry of Family. For just a split second, Amelia had forgotten the real reason she and Nick were marrying. She'd felt like a real bride—nervous, stressed, but a little bit excited, too. Nick's words brought her to earth in a hurry.

"Will the king be having dinner with us tonight?" Nick asked. "Maybe we can soften him up."

"He just ordered a meal to be brought to his room."

"A bit snobbish of him."

"I don't think it's that," Amelia said, surprised to be defending the king. "He looked awfully tired. I don't know what kind of work he does at the embassy every day, but it seems to take a lot out of him."

"Well, he is getting up there in years," Nick pointed out. "I'd better go see what the kids are up to before they flood the whole apartment."

DINNER WAS a strained affair, with just Charlotte, Amelia, Nick and the children. Charlotte had invited Nick, intending to get to know him better. But her getting-to-know-you conversation sounded more like an interrogation. Nick lost all sense of humor three minutes into the first course, but he answered the questions put to him.

The children, sensing tension, clammed up also despite Amelia's attempts to draw them out. Outwardly they might appear like normal children, but they were hypersensitive to negative undercurrents that they thought might threaten their newfound security.

Nick and the kids left immediately after dessert, and he made himself scarce over the next couple of days—for which she couldn't blame him. But was he avoiding Charlotte, or was he steering clear of Amelia?

"Don't worry about him, dear," Charlotte said. "Men avoid wedding plans like the plague." And the penthouse absolutely seethed with wedding plans. One couldn't turn around without running into a dressmaker, a caterer, a florist or a musician. The simple family wedding Amelia had envisioned had gotten completely out of hand. Though the guest list was still small, every detail received attention.

With the fairy-tale wedding plans all around her, it was easy to cast herself as the storybook princess marrying Prince Charming. But she knew the reality well enough. All she had to do was observe Nick studiously ignoring her to be reminded of his true priorities—of which husbandly devotion to her was not at the top.

If her family noticed an absence of attentiveness between her and Nick when they were together, they didn't comment. Nick was pleasant—charming, even—but in a detached sort of way. But there was a calm intensity about him, a quiet sadness just beneath the surface that one sensed ran deep, but he certainly didn't confide in her.

She couldn't fault his obvious devotion to his children. He wasn't overtly affectionate, but he paid them constant attention—gently correcting their table manners, encouraging them to try new foods, and most important, listening to them. He seemed to actually understand Jakob's conversations, even when the child retreated to baby talk, which he did when he was tired or upset.

She wondered what he'd been like with his first child. Had he been so attentive? Or had he been casually involved, leaving most of the child-rearing to his wife and running off to fight his wars? She would have liked to ask him. But there were some parts of Nick that were so unreachable, it was like staring down into a bottomless well.

ON FRIDAY EVENING, Amelia's hands shook as she put on her mother's pearl earrings, dressing for her wedding in her suite, preparing to marry a man she hardly knew. Yes, she'd spent time with him, but he showed her only what he wished her to see. There was no sense of trust, not even a glimmering hint that he might eventually confide in her.

She couldn't help but be apprehensive about Nicholas Standish being her husband—far more worried than she'd been when they married so hastily in Palemeir. Back then she hadn't realized the marriage wouldn't be legal, yet she'd jumped in eagerly with both feet.

Yuki helped her into the wedding gown, which Amelia had to admit was beautiful. The designer had almost miraculously captured the dream dress lurking in Amelia's imagination, and it fit her body perfectly. The décolletage was a bit more revealing than she was accustomed to—she normally downplayed the fact she was amply endowed. But her mother assured her the hint of cleavage shown by the dress was not in poor taste.

Amelia had decided not to wear a veil or hat, so her mother had hired a stylist to shape Amelia's blond curls into an elaborate do, woven through with baby's breath and a discreet tiara. The end effect—dress, hair, makeup—was far more pleasing than Amelia wanted to admit. She looked like a rather wanton goddess—and very bridelike, despite the less-than-traditional outfit.

"God, Amelia, you look fantastic." CeCe fussed with a mutinous curl sticking out over Amelia's ear.

"It's so *you*," Lucia added. "I'm glad you put your foot down and went with a dress that fits your personality."

"I had my doubts," Charlotte admitted, "but you are truly a vision. Nick will faint dead away when he sees you."

If that were only true. Amelia realized with a start that all of her preparations today were in the hope that she *would* impress Nick.

"Do you have any idea where Nick's taking you for the honeymoon?" CeCe asked as the hairdresser worked on her hair.

"Honeymoon?" Amelia repeated. "I guess I assumed we wouldn't have one. It takes time to prepare for a trip, especially when we have to take security measures." She shrugged.

"No honeymoon?" Lucia said. "Are you crazy?"

"She has a point," Charlotte said. "The public eye is on Amelia now, especially since—" She stopped herself.

"Especially since what?" Amelia asked.

"Well, I wasn't going to say anything because I didn't want to spoil your special day, but the press did finally catch on to the wedding story."

"Not Krissy Katwell, I hope."

"None other than," CeCe said. "You better just show it to her, Mother, or she'll pester us to death."

Charlotte left the room, and reappeared a few moments later with a section of the *Manhattan Chronicle,* which she handed wordlessly to Amelia.

"'Are those wedding bells we hear chiming from the royal penthouse?'" Amelia read aloud. "'With the ink on Princess Cecelia's marriage license hardly dry, I have it on impeccable authority that another member of the American royal family is tying the knot—for the second time.

"'Recently I reported that Princess Amelia was secretly wed to rough-and-tumble mercenary Nicholas Standish while on a relief mission in war-torn Palemeir. It turns out that particular wedding ceremony didn't pass muster with Amelia's royal grandfather, King Easton of Korosol, who is insisting Amelia wed her soldier of fortune in a proper ceremony, sanctioned by a man of the cloth.'"

"Where does she get this stuff?" Lucia asked no one in particular. "That's not the right story at all."

"I would love to get my hands on Katwell's source for ten seconds," CeCe said.

"'The hush-hush wedding takes place this evening in the privacy of the Carradigne penthouse,'" Amelia continued. "'The press is definitely not invited. What are you hiding, Princess Amelia?'"

Amelia threw down the paper. "I'd like to get hold of Krissy herself for ten seconds."

"Don't let it upset you, dear. The column says very little, and you were planning to announce the marriage at some point."

"I should have told a legitimate reporter first," Amelia said, "so Krissy wouldn't have a scoop."

"Put it out of your mind. Krissy and her readers are of little meaning to us."

Amelia shook off the bad feeling of reading about herself in Krissy's column. "You're right. It's forgotten."

The wedding planner sailed in, announcing that it was time for everyone to head downstairs to the terrace. "The king is on his way to be seated, and we don't want to keep His Majesty waiting, do we?"

A shiver of apprehension wiggled up Amelia's spine. The king had been disturbingly noncommunicative on the subject of Amelia's upcoming marriage. She wondered if he had any surprises up his sleeve.

NICK AND THE KIDS had been banished to an office on the second floor to prepare for the wedding. It was a very masculine room, dominated by the portrait of the late Prince Drake, Amelia's father. Nick wondered whether the imposing portrait was supposed to be a warning that he'd better take good care of the Princess Amelia—or else.

Nick straightened Jakob's bow tie for the hundredth time. The child kept tugging on it.

"Hold still one more second," Nick said. "There."

"I look just like you," Jakob said proudly.

He did at that. He wore a miniature tuxedo just like Nick's, and they'd both gotten haircuts for the occasion, military short. Anyone who saw them together would assume they were biological father and son.

"How are you doing, Josie?" he asked his daughter. "Ready for flower-girl duty?"

"I'm really too old to be a flower girl," Josie complained.

"But if you weren't a flower girl, you couldn't wear that dress, now, could you?" The dress had been the high point of the week for Josie, who was not at all sure about this wedding business. When a box from Lady Charlotte had arrived at their hotel and Nick had brought out the frothy pink dress, Josie had actually gotten excited.

"It's a princess dress," she'd declared as she'd locked herself in the bathroom to try it on. When she'd emerged a few minutes later wearing the dress, she'd gazed at herself in the mirror for several minutes.

"Do you think I look like a princess?" she'd asked.

"Very princessly," Nick had assured her. "Maybe even a queen."

"When you marry Auntie Mellie, I'll be a princess, won't I?"

Nick hadn't had the heart to tell her she wouldn't be. Though mature in many ways, she wouldn't understand that you had to have royal blood—or marry it—before anyone would declare you royalty.

Today she'd taken a bubble bath and dressed with care. She'd sat still as stone while the hairdresser wove her golden curls into a grown-up twist woven with little white flowers. She might not be too sure about accepting Amelia as her mother, but she loved this princess stuff.

Nick wasn't sure how he felt about marrying Amelia, either. He'd deliberately avoided her this week, seeing her only twice, and with her family around. But he couldn't think straight when she was near. He appreciated what she was doing for him, but he wanted to be clear in his own mind how he would handle the marriage. They had studiously avoided talking about the future, but they would have to live as husband and wife, or at least appear to do so, for a short while.

Though he really, really wanted to make love to her, he suspected that wouldn't happen. She'd dashed his hopes where that was concerned the last time they'd married, and he wasn't expecting anything this time. Besides, this time he knew they wouldn't stay married. No sense in getting used to sleeping with the princess if he would eventually have to give it up.

Despite Amelia's fears, the king had done nothing to discourage him from marrying above his station. It looked as if the wedding would go off without a hitch—in a matter of minutes, if his watch was correct.

"Guess we better get going," he said. "Josie, you'd better go to Amelia's room with the rest of the bridesmaids."

"Okay. Uncle Nick?"

"Yes, Josie?"

"Good luck."

"Thank you." He would need it. He sent Josie on her way, then took Jakob's hand and led him down the back stairs and through the Grand Room to the terrace, which had been transformed into a fairyland of greenery, flowers and tiny white lights.

"Uncle Nick, your hand is all wet," Jakob said, pulling his hand out of Nick's grasp and wiping it on his tux pants.

So it was.

He couldn't be nervous. This wasn't a real marriage. He and Amelia needed only to playact for a few days, just long enough to make it look good for the Ministry of Family. Then they would separate and, after a decent interval, divorce, just as planned. So why were his palms sweating?

It was the tux. He'd never worn one, and he felt damn ridiculous. The sight of himself in the mirror had given him a start. He *looked* like a bridegroom.

As he greeted the few people he knew here, he couldn't help drawing comparisons to his first wedding—the one to Monette. Although their wedding ceremony had been quite informal, with the groom wearing his uniform and the bride in a Sunday dress, they'd married in a garden much like this. It was the smell of roses that brought back the memories.

He'd managed to escape his memories of Monette and William since he'd come to America. *Too busy,* he thought with a pang of guilt. Why did he have to think of them now? This ceremony was a mockery of the one he'd shared with his beautiful wife. Theirs had been a marriage steeped in love and commitment, the simple wedding a reflection of the purity of their feelings for one another.

Nick swallowed back the thickness in his throat. Now was not the time to be maudlin. He would get through this charade somehow.

There were only a few guests milling about the terrace before the ceremony, since the invitations had been limited to family and close friends, but the ones who were present were decked out to the nines. Nick's sister was here, of course, looking a bit dowdy among the royal finery in her very proper suit.

Several members of the royal guard were present, and various servants. The wedding planner flitted about here and there, making sure the roses weren't wilting and the reception buffet was in tip-top shape.

The king was not in evidence, but Nick imagined he meant to make an entrance that would rival Amelia's.

"How are you holding up?" Ellie asked as she straightened his white rose boutonniere. "I've never seen you look quite so handsome."

"Not even when I married Monette?" The words slipped out, and he immediately regretted them. This was supposed to be a happy occasion. He might still be miffed at Amelia for indirectly causing his custody woes, but she'd gone to a lot of trouble to make things right, and he had no cause to spoil the event with his dark thoughts.

"I wondered if you were thinking about Monette," Ellie said. "You looked a bit sad just now."

"I'm fine."

"She would have wanted this," Ellie said. "She wouldn't want you to mourn forever."

That was true. For Ellie's sake, Nick smiled. He was supposed to be the happy bridegroom, anticipating being joined with the woman he loved. He'd not told anyone, even Eleanor, the truth about his and Amelia's arrangement. Ellie was a terrible liar, and some snooping social worker was bound to question her about this spur-of-the-moment ceremony. Best if she believed it was a love match, at least for now.

"Who is that guy?" he asked Ellie, nodding toward a slightly balding, slightly overweight man close to his own age, or maybe a bit older.

"You're joking, right? That's Prince Markus. He's just come back from Europe."

"My God, you're right. He's aged since I last saw him. Who's that guy with him?"

"That's Winston Rademacher, his right-hand man.

Not a very nice fellow, if you ask me, but he's utterly devoted to Markus, and vice versa. He's been very supportive this past year. Markus's parents' deaths have been very hard on him.''

''His lifestyle is what's been hard on him, if you ask me.''

''He's changed a lot since the accident,'' Ellie remarked. ''He's much more serious, not the playboy he used to be.''

''He's on his best behavior, I imagine, since he's heir to the throne now. Still, there's always hope Easton will come to his senses and declare some other family member as his heir. Don't the laws of succession in Korosol give him that option?''

Eleanor cleared her throat. ''Um, yes. I believe so.''

''Maybe he'll choose Amelia,'' Nick said dryly. ''I'd make some royal consort, don't you think?''

Eleanor cleared her throat again.

''Ellie, are you coming down with a cold?''

''Yes, I might be. I'd better go see what's keeping the king.'' She scooted away from him like a whipped dog, making him wonder if he'd said something to upset or offend her. Perhaps she hadn't appreciated his negative comments about Markus. He hoped she wasn't fostering a crush on Korosol's future king.

As seven o'clock approached, the king made his appearance without any pomp and circumstance. He was shown to a place of honor in the front row, next to Lady Charlotte, and the rest of the assembled guests found chairs. He then proceeded to stare intensely straight at Nick. Nick could have read disapproval in his gaze, but it actually felt more as if the monarch was sizing him up, evaluating his worth as a grandson-in-law.

Nick nodded an acknowledgment as if to say, *I won't hurt her.* Reverend Baker took his place in front and motioned for Nick to stand with him. Nick's apprehension grew. It might be a marriage of convenience, but right now it felt awfully real.

The string quartet started with a classical piece Nick recognized but couldn't name, something from Bach, maybe. Amelia's sisters marched one at a time down the aisle with solemn faces. They wore pastel dresses, similar but not identical. Still, with their hair styled the same, Nick could see the family resemblance for the first time. The princesses were all uncommonly beautiful women.

His own Josie came down the aisle next, sprinkling white rose petals from a basket and taking her task very seriously. She *did* look like a princess. She came to stand beside CeCe and Lucia, and she smiled shyly at Nick.

Nothing had prepared Nick for the sight of Amelia, however. The small assemblage issued a collective sigh when she appeared, dressed in flowing silk, wearing a tiara, and clutching a huge bouquet of white and purple flowers. She could have been the cover girl for one of those bride's magazines.

It was her face that did him in. She looked scared. Surely she wasn't frightened of him. He intended to be the most undemanding of husbands. She wouldn't even have to deal with him during the next couple of weeks if she didn't want to. They could live in the penthouse, where there was so much room they could conceivably live for weeks without contact.

But she was definitely trembling.

He felt compassion for her welling up inside him, and the enormity of her sacrifice suddenly hit him. A short-lived marriage was no big deal to him, his jitters of a few minutes ago notwithstanding. It would have little impact on his future, other than to assure him he'd get to keep his kids. But for a woman like Amelia, in the highbrow circles she moved in, a failed marriage was a huge deal. She was tainting herself. And if she married again, she wouldn't wear white.

For Amelia, this wedding was it, the pinnacle of her princessly existence.

She didn't make eye contact with him as she glided up the aisle, looking like an angel—an angel with fabulous breasts. The gown showed more of her chest than Nick was accustomed to seeing. And what a terribly irreverent thought to have at a moment like this.

He tried to catch her eye, but she kept her gaze focused on the minister.

The ceremony itself went quickly. Nick remembered little of what was said. There had been no rehearsal, so the minister prompted them through their vows. Nick's voice shook when he got to the part about "as long as we both shall live." When Amelia got to that part, her voice lowered to an almost whisper.

"May the Lord bless the union of Nicholas and Amelia," the minister intoned, "brought together in wartime, united by their concern for children, nurturing their love amidst hardships few of us will ever know. But a rose planted in rock can grow and bloom, if given water and sun, if nurtured and pruned. May the love you share also grow and thrive despite hardships, past and future.

"I now pronounce you husband and wife."

Finally, Amelia looked at him, her eyes huge and luminous, reflecting the greenery all around them, and the guests held a collective breath. This was where he was supposed to kiss the bride, he realized.

Why hadn't he anticipated this moment sooner? He and Amelia had kissed exactly once before, at the airport in Palemeir. And he'd nearly fainted from it.

She leaned slightly toward him. He took her in his arms and touched his lips to hers, very lightly, very respectfully. Her lips were cool and dry, but he felt the tiny influx of breath as their mouths made contact.

He pulled away as quickly as he dared.

"I present to you Mr. and Mrs. Nicholas Standish," the minister said, and the guests applauded. They both turned to face their family and friends.

"Smile," Nick whispered to her. "You look like a deer on railroad tracks with a freight train barreling toward it."

She did smile, but she whispered back, "Thanks. I'll always remember those were the first words you spoke to me as my real husband."

Chapter Seven

Easton struggled not to smile. The wedding ceremony had been amazingly touching. He knew Amelia and Nicholas weren't in love, but probably no one else could have figured it out by watching them.

Especially if they'd paid close attention to that kiss. Not the steamy, practiced kiss of experienced lovers, or the perfunctory kiss of friends, but the tentative kiss of anticipation, of new feelings, maybe a bit of apprehension. Everything a new bride and groom *should* be experiencing.

He only wished the press had captured this moment. The citizens of his home country would lap it up with a spoon when this hit the newspapers in Korosol—especially if he had Eleanor feed a few tidbits to some key reporters. Not that dreadful Krissy Katwell, though. She would find a way to twist the facts and embarrass his family yet again.

Everyone was heading to the Grand Room, where a huge banquet table was loaded down with every sort of delicacy imaginable. He'd noticed it on the way to the terrace. Too bad he couldn't enjoy most of it. He missed all the rich foods he used to indulge in, but doctor's orders were doctor's orders.

Charlotte slipped up beside him. "Easton, walk with me to the reception, will you?"

"Delighted."

"It was a lovely ceremony, don't you think?"

"It seemed to suit Amelia," he said with deliberate evasiveness. When the time was right, he would reveal his opinion about the recent nuptials. Not before. He wanted the future queen to stew in her juices a while longer. She had defied him, and he didn't want to encourage that. But he wouldn't want Korosol's head of state to be some shrinking violet who caved in the first time some overbearing man raised his voice.

In light of the casual nature of the wedding, there was no formal receiving line. But the bride and groom stood near the buffet, sipping champagne and accepting well wishes.

"Would you like to pay them your respects?" Charlotte asked carefully. "I'm sure it would mean a great deal to them."

"In a few minutes, when things are calmer," Easton said. "First I'd like to get something to drink."

"Of course. I ordered your favorite champagne." She reached for a glass from the tray of a passing waiter, but Easton halted her.

"Not champagne, though your thoughtfulness is appreciated. Might I have some mineral water?" He would have asked for milk if he'd thought it wouldn't arouse his daughter-in-law's concern. Those cursed pills he had to take night and day played havoc with his stomach—and didn't mix well with alcohol.

Charlotte stopped a passing waiter and whispered

in his ear. Moments later, Easton had a cold glass of Perrier in his hand.

The minister stopped to talk to Charlotte, distracting her for long enough that Easton could pop his pills. He stepped behind a huge potted fern, pulled a small vial from his pocket, emptied his evening dosage into his hand and tossed the pills into his mouth. He washed the whole lot down with his mineral water, swallowed with a grimace—and realized Charlotte was right there, staring at him.

"That must be some headache," she commented.

"Yes, a very bad one indeed," Easton said, forcing a smile. "Nothing a bit of aspirin won't fix."

"That wasn't aspirin."

"Of course it was. Why would you think it wasn't?"

Charlotte gave him a look that said she wanted to challenge him. He gave her a look right back that said he wouldn't tolerate any further questions. He wouldn't discuss his health problems until Korosol's future was safely deposited into the hands of his successor.

"Let's go get something to eat, shall we?" He took Charlotte's arm and led her toward the buffet.

"I can have someone fill a plate for you, if you'd like to sit down," Charlotte said.

"Nonsense. I've been smelling this buffet for several minutes now. I want to pick out my own choices." He did, selecting a bit of smoked salmon and steamed vegetables, a spoonful of rice, and fresh fruit for dessert, bypassing a gorgeous-looking custard and chocolate truffles, as well as his favorite brandy.

Just as he was about to set his plate on the table, a small whirlwind in a pink dress plowed right into him, nearly knocking him off his feet and causing his plate to jostle, sending his broccoli sailing through the air. Charlotte, still hovering, steadied him, then turned to Josie.

"Josie, I believe an apology is in order."

Josie looked up at Easton, her eyes filled with fear. "I'm sorry, sir. I mean, Your Majesty. I didn't look where I was going."

He was once again impressed by the girl's solemn formality. Now that he knew more about her, thanks to Harrison's exhaustive research on the life of Nicholas Standish, he felt far more compassion for her than on their first meeting.

"It's quite all right, my dear," he said, giving her a kindly smile. "This is a party, after all, and we're supposed to be having fun."

She dropped a quick curtsy. "Yes, Your Majesty. May I go now?"

"Yes, run along." As she walked off at a sedate pace, posture erect, shoulders tense, he wished he could do something to ease her pain. And she was in pain. She might hide it well, but he was a shrewd judge of body language. He turned to Charlotte. "She is a very charming child."

He sat down to enjoy his ascetic meal.

"Easton," Charlotte said, "won't you say something to Amelia?"

"I intend to say quite a few things to the Princess Amelia," he said. "All in good time. See to your other guests. I'm fine for the time being."

Easton started to feel a little guilty over the game he played with his granddaughter. He took a few bites of the salmon, which he knew had been flown in last night from Alaska, but it could have been sawdust for all he could taste. A few more bites, a bit of conversation with Ellie, who had been seated beside him, and he pushed his plate away.

He'd let this game go too far. Best to set things right.

The bride and groom were finding their seats at the table across from him. Amelia caught his eye, giving him a questioning look. He frowned and pushed back from the table, then very deliberately walked around the table and behind Amelia. He bent down and whispered in her ear. Then he announced to the room at large, "Forgive me for stealing the bride away for a few minutes."

With a longing look toward her plate, which appeared to contain the same health-conscious choices he'd made, Amelia rose from her chair and followed Easton out of the Grand Room and up the back stairs to her father's private office, which had been left nearly unchanged since his death.

Easton sat in a red leather chair, and invited Amelia to sit, also. "You make a lovely bride."

"Thank you, Grandfather."

"There is something we need to discuss."

"I know. I'm so sorry to have displeased you. Under the circumstances, you'll of course have to choose another heir. You can't have a queen married to a former mercenary, especially not with two adopted children. I just wanted you to know that, while I'm disappointed, I understand completely."

"You have it all wrong, my dear."

"I do?"

"While I was initially distressed over news of your marriage, I did some checking up on Nicholas Standish."

"You did?"

"Yes, technically he was working as a mercenary, a soldier of fortune. But that doesn't mean he could be hired by any country to do anything. He was quite selective in his assignments. His work leaned heavily toward peacekeeping—restoring order where there was unrest and instability, protecting vulnerable populations, relief efforts—like the one in Palemeir. He's also been involved in counterterrorism activities—most of these top secret, so even my best man was unable to get much information."

Amelia nodded. That was more than *she* knew about Nick.

"But his activities have been completely honorable. I couldn't find anyone to speak ill of the man. He never went around killing people willy-nilly like some out-of-control Mambo."

"I think you mean Rambo."

"Right. The point is, your Nick is no ordinary war hero. As a member of the Korosol Armed Forces, he was part of the peacekeeping force in Kosovo, where he was wounded by sniper fire."

Amelia gasped. "He was shot?"

Easton nodded. "He received the Korosol Cross of Bravery, the equivalent of the American Congressional Medal of Honor. He requested an honorable discharge, and got it, when his wife and child died. Since then, he's been involved in one heroic effort after another. He might not be of royal birth, or even in the top echelon of society, but I can't imagine a more fitting prince for Korosol's future queen."

"No kidding?" Amelia blurted out.

"As for those children, who could possibly object to them? War orphans, adopted so they could escape the dangers of their battle-torn country and have a better life. Granted, an adopted child could not inherit the throne. But there's plenty of time for you and Nicholas to bear biological children of your own.''

''Yes, plenty of time.''

''My dear, are you feeling all right? You seem awfully pale.''

''Just the excitement of the wedding,'' she said. ''And you did pull me away from my dinner before I could eat a bite.''

Cheeky girl. She would charm Korosol to pieces.

''Now, then,'' he said, ''I trust I've put your mind at ease about your future.''

''Oh, yes, completely. Thank you for…for being so understanding.''

''Go to your husband now. I think I'd like to sit in here a while longer and remember my son. This room makes me feel very close to him.''

''Yes, it does me, too,'' Amelia said as she rose. ''Good evening.''

AMELIA FELT a few moments of elation, followed by a quick plummet to despair that had her returning to the Grand Room on shaky legs. She hadn't ruined her chances to be queen. Her act of defiance hadn't gotten her in trouble with the king after all. If anything, he was even more pleased with his choice of heir.

But now she had a new problem. How was she going to break the news to Nick? He would not take it well, that much she knew. He was not the royal-consort type. And if a discreet divorce had been unlikely before, surely now it would be impossible. When Easton made his announcement, *nothing* she did would be discreet.

She hadn't imagined in a million years that she would face this particular dilemma. Nick was counting on that quick, painless divorce.

She pasted on a smile and returned to the dining table.

"What was that about?" Nick wanted to know.

"Oh, just my grandfather being melodramatic. He wanted to congratulate me privately."

"And not me?"

Amelia suspected Nick would get his share of royal attention. The king would no doubt expect Nick to undertake the same sort of tutoring she was currently enduring, to ensure he understood his duties and responsibilities as husband to the queen. Including that bit about having children.

Oh, heaven help her, she'd made a real mess of things.

She looked over at Lucia, who was seated next to her, digging in to a plate full of delicacies Amelia couldn't even look at without gaining weight.

"You're in big trouble," she whispered to her sister.

Lucia's eyes widened. "Oh, God, he's not choosing me, is he? I mean, that's impossible."

"No. He's sticking with me. Your plan backfired."

Lucia smiled. "Really?"

"He thinks Nick will make a great royal consort."

"Then I think you're the one who's in trouble. How's Nick taking it?"

"He doesn't know. I haven't told him about the queen thing yet."

"You're definitely in trouble."

"I intend to make you pay for getting me into this."

"Don't be ridiculous. You're married to a gorgeous hunk, and you've got an instant family, to boot. Life couldn't be sweeter."

"Are you forgetting? It's not a real marriage."

"So who says you can't make it real?" Lucia said with an impish smile.

So who says you can't make it real? That phrase bounced around in Amelia's head for the remainder of the reception, which seemed to go on for hours and hours. Last time she'd listened to Lucia, it had gotten her *into* this mess. So why was she even considering her younger sister's advice now?

Maybe because the idea had been flitting around in her own head before Lucia had said a word. It wouldn't be so bad to stay married to Nick, to be a mother to those children. She already cared for him, respected him, and she knew he at least had the capacity to be fond of her. Couldn't that grow into love?

As for the physical aspects, she'd been fantasizing about Nick's body since the first moment she saw him at the Palemeir refugee camp, standing in his underwear in the open-air shower, which essentially consisted of a bucket of water suspended overhead. He'd pulled on a rope, emptying the bucket's sun-warmed rainwater over him, and she'd watched in awe as the water had drenched his wavy, dark blond hair and sluiced over his granite-hard body.

Then one of the kids had stolen his towel, and he'd chased after the perpetrator with mock fury. When he'd caught the boy, they'd engaged in a spirited game of tug-of-war until Nick had finally regained his towel. The child had scampered off, leaving Nick standing in the mud clearing drying himself off, wearing that pensive, sad look she now understood—and not much else.

So who says you can't make it real? Nick, for one. He didn't want to be married to her, or anyone. From what Ellie had told her, he was still in love with Monette, his deceased wife, and was loath to betray her memory. And even if Amelia could win him over, which she wasn't sure she wanted to do, he would drop her like a hot potato once he learned about the queen thing. Living in the public eye was anathema to the quiet life he wanted to live with the children.

Well, first things first. She had to figure out how to get through the wedding night. Amazingly, she and Nick had not discussed plans for the immediate future. Amelia had tried to bring up the subject, but he kept telling her not to worry, it would work out.

The festivities were winding down now. The king had long since retired, and Markus and that shifty-looking friend of his, Rademacher, had left at the first opportunity. The wedding cake was nothing but a sad little lump of crumbs and icing, and the caviar was depleted. The moment of reckoning had arrived.

Amelia located Charlotte, who was chatting with Ellie.

"Mother, if I have to stand one more minute in these shoes, I'll break down in tears."

Charlotte glanced at her watch. "Oh, my, yes, look at the time. Why don't you go slip into your going-away outfit."

"I'm not actually sure we're going anywhere. I thought we could hang out here."

Charlotte looked horrified. "You're spending your wedding night here?"

"We never got around to making honeymoon

plans. There was just too much to do.'' CeCe hadn't planned a honeymoon either, Amelia recalled. But Shane had spirited her away after the wedding. That had been so romantic. Amelia doubted Nick could be counted on for a gesture like that. ''And there are the children to think about. Who would take care of them if we ran off someplace?''

''You know perfectly well Hester would jump through hoops for the chance to care for those children. Oh, Amelia, you *have* to have a honeymoon.''

''We haven't made reservations anyplace. It's all right, really. We'll catch our breath, and then we'll figure something out.''

''Nonsense. Go change clothes. I've got an idea.''

Oh, dear. Once Charlotte got hold of an idea, she was like a goat butting a fence post. Amelia went to Nick. ''Mother wants me to change into my going-away outfit. She's got some sort of plan in mind for our honeymoon. Be prepared for anything.''

''If you're changing clothes, I'm changing. And as God is my witness, I'll never wear a tuxedo again.''

''You look gorgeous in it.''

''You have to say that. You're my wife.''

''I'm not likely to forget that fact anytime soon.''

Amelia passed through the foyer on her way to the front stairs. One of the downstairs guards emerged from the elevator just as she passed.

''Princess Amelia. This telegram just arrived for you and Mr. Standish.''

''Thank you, Walt.'' She took the envelope from him, overcome with curiosity. A telegram? How quaint. Someone offering congratulations, no doubt, though she couldn't imagine who. She decided she and Nick should read it together, so she didn't open it right away.

In the sanctuary of her room, she took a moment to just sit in a chair and relax her tense muscles. She was married. That fact had seemed more real in Palemeir, when the wedding wasn't even legal. In Palemeir, she hadn't felt like some counterfeit princess bride going through the motions. Then again, everything seemed more real when she was on a relief mission. Sometimes she got the feeling her life in New York was just a fairy tale.

Amelia hadn't selected a going-away outfit. She pawed through her closet, locating a simple blue dress that was one of her favorites. She matched it with a pair of white sandals that laced around the ankle.

And a suitcase. She hadn't packed for a honeymoon because she'd figured there wouldn't be one. As accustomed as she was to taking off for exotic locales at a moment's notice, or vacating a camp when danger threatened, she could pack a bag of essentials in under thirty seconds. She did that now, including some comfortable clothes and two bestselling paperbacks she'd been wanting to read. She figured she and Nick wouldn't have anything else to do on a honeymoon.

Unless... No, that wasn't what they'd agreed to. Lucia's advice be damned.

When Amelia returned downstairs, Nick had already changed clothes and reappeared. He was even faster than her.

"There you are," Charlotte said, beaming. "Can I have your attention, everyone? Everyone?" Charlotte tapped her knife on a glass, and the guests quieted down. "Given the hasty nature of the wedding preparations, Nick and Amelia didn't have time to plan a honeymoon. But I have a solution. The DeLacey Shipping corporate yacht isn't being used at the moment. So I got on the phone and assembled a skeleton crew for the boat—they're on their way to the marina as we speak, and they're at your disposal for two weeks.

"Amelia and Nick, please allow me to give you a proper honeymoon as my wedding present to you."

Amelia stifled a gasp. She looked at Nick, but the only clue that the news didn't meet with his complete approval was a muscle ticking in his cheek.

"Lady Charlotte," Nick said, "that is most generous of you. The honeymoon is supposed to be the groom's responsibility, and I confess I fell down on the job. In fact, I wasn't even sure how to proceed with planning a wedding trip, given the necessary security measures to protect Princess Amelia."

Oh, baloney, Amelia thought. Nick was a tactical genius. He could have planned ten honeymoons over the past week if he'd wanted to. He just hadn't wanted to.

"Thank you, Mother," Amelia managed to say. "I haven't sailed in years. I'm sure we'll enjoy it."

"We get to go on a boat?" Josie asked excitedly, which produced a titter of laughter from the guests.

CeCe stepped in to answer the question. "This trip is for grown-ups only, Josie," she gently explained. "But while your uncle Nick and auntie Mellie are gone, you can stay here with me and your uncle Shane, and Hester and Quincy and Grandma Charlotte."

Charlotte fanned herself at the mention of "Grandma" attached to her name.

"Won't that be fun?" CeCe continued.

Josie did not look as if she thought staying at the penthouse without her uncle Nick would be at all fun. "But I want to go on the boat."

"We'll take the children with us," Nick declared.

"Of course we will," Amelia quickly agreed. "A honeymoon is for the bride and groom to get to know each other better, but I need to get to know the children, too." And the children would provide a convenient buffer between her and Nick. And with the crew hanging around, she and Nick would probably never have to be alone—perfect conditions for helping her avoid temptation.

"The limo is waiting downstairs, whenever you're ready," Charlotte said.

"Let me pack a couple of bags for me and the kids, and we'll be ready, too," Nick said cheerfully. A little too cheerfully, Amelia thought.

Everyone applauded, and Charlotte looked very satisfied with herself.

"I'll help you," Amelia said, following Nick out of the Grand Room toward the office where he'd stowed his belongings.

As soon as they were out of earshot of the guests, Amelia brought up the real reason she'd followed him. "Are you okay with this? I had nothing to do with it. My mother, as always, has her own ideas about how to do things."

"I'm fine with it. The kids will have a blast."

But what about us? she wanted to ask. On a luxurious yacht, with nothing to do but laze in the sun and breathe in fresh ocean breezes, who knew what could happen?

Who says you can't make it real?

But Amelia was forgetting something. She hadn't been honest with Nick about her future as queen of Korosol. Until she crossed that hurdle, she and Nick didn't have a chance of forming any kind of lasting bond. But she was very afraid that when Nick found out what she'd kept from him, they *really* wouldn't have a chance.

"Oh, Nick, we received a telegram a while ago."

Nick paused in the act of rolling up clothes and stashing them into a couple of duffel bags. "Really? From whom? Who sends telegrams anymore?"

"I don't know. I waited to open it so we could do it together." She pulled the thin envelope from her dress pocket and used her father's brass letter opener to slit the top. She extracted the paper inside and unfolded it. Unfortunately, it was in French, which she had never mastered in school. The king had been tutoring her in the language, however, so she gave translation her best shot:

"'For Princess Amelia Carradigne Standish and Mr. Nicholas Standish—Congratulations on your recent nuptials. We are pleased to see you are… something, something…to give Josie and Jakob a stable home environment.'"

Nick looked up. "Who's that from?"

Amelia scanned down the page. "There's no name, just the Ministry of Family."

"I'll be damned."

"There's more." She continued reading. "'However, given the transitory nature of your first wedding, we are…concerned about your motives—'"

"I'll just bet they are."

"'As you know, our policies do not support marriages…something, something…to facilitate adoption.'''

"Yes, I'm familiar with their wretched policy."

"'Therefore, we take active interest in the veracity of this marriage. Should you habitate as husband and wife…something, something—'''

"What?"

"It's in French." She handed him the telegram.

Nick took up where she left off. "'Should you habitate as husband and wife for a sufficient period of time to indicate that the marriage is legitimate, we will be pleased to award you permanent custody of Josie and Jakob.'''

Amelia gasped. "Sufficient period—how long is that?"

Nick studied the telegram again. When he looked up his face had gone pale. "Six months."

Chapter Eight

"Six months!" Amelia repeated.

"That's half a *year*," Nick said, sounding horrified.

"Well, you needn't make it seem like a death sentence."

"I'm just dumbfounded, that's all. What am I supposed to do with you for six months?"

Amelia could have answered that in a number of creative ways, all of them inappropriate for family viewing. She immediately shut down that line of thinking.

"We can't stay in America the whole time," Nick said. "I have to get Josie back in school. I've been tutoring her as best I can, but she's already a year behind."

"They have schools in New York. The spring term is almost over anyway. We could enroll her in any number of excellent summer programs here in Manhattan. She's an extremely intelligent child. They could have her up to her appropriate grade level in no time."

"Are you saying you don't want to go to Korosol with me?" he asked point-blank.

"I'll go. Just…not right now. My sister is having a baby. I want to be around for that." And pretty soon she would be living in Korosol on a permanent basis. She only had a short time left with her family, and she wanted to take advantage of it.

"I was hoping to get the children home and settled as soon as possible," Nick said. "They need consistency, and a routine."

"They have consistency—you. And they don't seem to be suffering too many ill effects from moving around. I think it's great you want to bring them on our honeymoon."

"You do?"

"Sure. I meant what I said. I want to spend time with them, get to know them better."

"So you can abandon them when the six months is over."

"We'll explain it to them."

"They won't understand. Jakob, especially, is too young to comprehend why you're leaving. It would be better if you didn't get close to them at all."

"What am I supposed to do, ignore them for the next six months? Unless you want to chuck this whole plan, we're all stuck together. I intend to make the best of it."

Nick sighed. "You're right. These aren't the best circumstances, but they're the ones we're stuck with. And besides, six months isn't that long, in the grand scheme of things. We'll survive somehow."

"Thanks for the vote of confidence." He hadn't even realized he'd insulted her with the sentiment he'd voiced. The idea that six months with her was something to be *survived* wasn't the highest compliment she'd ever been paid.

"What's that?" Amelia asked, pointing to a small gold picture frame Nick was about to wrap inside a shirt.

"It's my wife and son." He made no move to show her the picture, just rolled the shirt around it and stuck it in his duffel. "And just for the record, that subject is not open for discussion," he continued. "My loss is not something to be exposed to the light and prodded. It's not something I need to 'talk out' so I can understand it better. I don't need you to help me 'get over it.' Are we clear on that?"

"Crystal." *And excuse me for living.* She must have been crazy to even briefly entertain the idea that she could make this a real marriage. Nick wasn't exactly an ogre, but he was not about to open up to her and trust her in any meaningful way. Trust was essential to any marriage. Without it, they had nothing more than an uneasy business alliance. "Shall we return to our guests and pretend to be a devoted husband and wife?"

"I'm ready."

She shook her head and followed him out of the room.

NICK COULDN'T WAIT until his nuptial celebration was over. Not that Amelia's family wasn't perfectly nice, despite their royal blood. He'd actually enjoyed outspoken Lucia, and Josie adored CeCe, who had come to embody the concept of a real live princess in the little girl's mind. All of them doted on Jakob. Even the king wasn't so bad.

"I'm so pleased for you, Nicky," Ellie said as she gave him a hug. "Amelia will be very good for you. I can see she's changed you for the better already."

"And just exactly what was wrong with me before?"

"Oh, you know what I mean. You're smiling more."

He was a very good actor, that was all. Being married to Amelia did not make him want to smile. In fact, he felt distinctly disloyal to Monette's memory as the wedding guests pelted him and Amelia with rice in the posh apartment building's lobby. Though it had been years, he could still hear Monette's squeal of laughter as their guests had done the same thing. This wedding had brought back too many painful memories.

He ushered Josie and Jakob into the limo, then Amelia, who turned and waved to a couple of photographers who had gotten wind of the wedding and camped outside. The Carradignes had decided a few carefully orchestrated wedding photos in the press wouldn't be a bad thing.

Just before Amelia ducked into the car, Lucia ran up and pressed something into Amelia's hand, then whispered something in her ear. Amelia blushed, swatted her sister, then climbed into the back seat. Whatever Lucia had given Amelia was gone by the time Nick joined her.

When the door was slammed shut by Amelia's bodyguard, the limo suddenly became blissfully quiet. A pane of glass separated them from the driver and Jules, the bodyguard who'd been assigned to accompany them.

The driver knew where to go. Josie and Jakob, up well past their bedtime, quickly dozed off despite the novelty of riding in a limousine.

Nick and Amelia were silent.

She gazed out the tinted windows at the city lights of Manhattan, giving him the opportunity to study her without her noticing. She did not look happy, as a bride should. She unconsciously twisted the plain gold band he'd given her as a wedding ring. Maybe he should have gotten something a bit fancier. She was a princess, after all. But at the time he'd purchased the ring, it hadn't seemed sensible to spend a lot of money on a ring that would be worn so briefly. He suspected, though, that it wasn't the cost of the ring that made her unhappy. It was the groom. He'd been less than gracious toward her this whole week.

It wasn't that he didn't appreciate the sacrifice she was making on his behalf. He needed to get it out of his head that the mess he was in was all her fault. She was turning her life upside down to help him and his kids. It was time he acknowledged that.

"Tired?" he asked.

"A bit keyed up, actually. I hope this business with the DeLacey yacht didn't throw you for a loop. Mother was trying to help."

"I'm sure it will be fine."

"We don't have to stay on board for long. We can always claim seasickness. That's what happened to poor CeCe on *her* honeymoon, so she set a precedent."

"The vice president of DeLacey Shipping gets seasick?" Nick found that highly amusing.

"I know, it's ironic."

"We'll play it by ear. We'll have to be careful where the kids are concerned. They both can swim like fish, but that wouldn't help much if one of them toppled off in the middle of the ocean."

Amelia shivered. "First thing we'll do once on board is check for child-size life jackets."

"How big is this crew your mother summoned?"

"She told me a captain and first mate. Plus Jules, for security, and he's agreed to pitch in where he's needed."

"You mean the gorilla in the front seat?"

"He's very nice."

"Do we really need all those people? I mean, I can handle a boat."

Amelia just smiled. He soon learned why as the limousine pulled into the marina, Liberty Landing, just on the other side of the Holland Tunnel in Liberty State Park. The driver parked in a lot. They all piled out and grabbed a piece of luggage as they were hoofing it from there.

Nick carried Jakob in addition to one of the duffel bags. He held tightly to Josie's hand.

"These boats are huge," Josie commented. "Is ours one of these?"

"Down a little farther," Amelia answered. When they finally stopped, it was in front of the biggest private yacht he'd ever seen. It might even have been bigger than the king's.

"Holy…" Nick didn't have words to describe it.

"It's a ship!" Josie said delightedly. "Uncle Nick, look at the name."

"Duchess," he said, reading the name off the side of the boat. "Not princess?"

"Mother is duchess of Avion," Amelia explained.

As the two other crew members paused from their activities to carry luggage onto the yacht, Nick could see why a woman would feel like a princess here. No luxury had been overlooked on the sleek, white craft, from teak decks to inch-thick carpets in the saloon to state-of-the-art kitchen and bathrooms that would look at home in any four-star hotel.

"This is unbelievable," Nick murmured.

"Where would you like your things?" asked Dave, the first mate.

"Let's put the kids together in the Blue Cabin. It's right next door to the owner's suite. You can put my things in the—"

Nick loudly cleared his throat. "You mean *our* things."

A look of alarm crossed Amelia's face before she quickly masked it. "Of course. This being-married stuff will take getting used to. Put our things in the owner's suite."

Dave, a small, very energetic man close to Nick's own thirty years, saluted while smiling indulgently. "Yes, Princess."

Amelia turned to Nick. "Let's get the kiddos to bed, huh? They're zonked."

"I want to look around," Josie protested.

"Tomorrow," Nick said. "You'll have plenty of time to explore, don't worry. And Josie, I don't want you or Jakob on deck without a life jacket and an adult present. I'll expect you to help watch your brother."

"Okay," she said through a yawn.

"I'm not kidding about this."

She gave him a curious look. "Okay."

The Blue Cabin featured twin berths and had its own little bathroom attached. Nick laid a sleeping Jakob onto one of the beds and started undressing him.

"Let's get you into some pajamas, okay?" Amelia said to Josie.

"I can dress myself, thank you," Josie said primly. She took her little suitcase and disappeared into the bathroom.

Amelia sighed. Nick wanted to offer her words of encouragement. Josie was a hard nut to crack, and she was moody. Sometimes she snuggled up to Nick like a puppy, and sometimes she didn't want anything to do with him. With time, Josie would warm to Amelia.

But the words didn't come. He still had grave reservations about Amelia worming her way into his children's affections. He just wasn't sure it would be good for them in the long run.

Josie emerged in a nightgown a few minutes later and crawled under the covers of her berth. Jakob was already asleep.

"Good night, Josie." Nick straightened the covers over her frail body.

"'Night, Uncle Nick."

"Good night, Josie," Amelia echoed. "Thank you for being such a good flower girl."

Josie didn't respond. Whether she'd already fallen asleep, or she was just being snotty, he wasn't sure.

Now that the little ones were tucked in, it was time to worry about the grown-ups' sleeping arrangements. Nick and Amelia entered the owner's suite together. It was incredibly opulent and surprisingly roomy. Nick would never have guessed he was on a boat if not for the gentle rocking beneath his feet.

"I feel almost guilty, sleeping in a place like this," he said.

"I know what you mean. Quite a step up from that refugee camp where we met."

Nick opened the bathroom door and peeked into

the marble and glass wonderland. ''I bet the shower's an improvement, too.''

Amelia averted her gaze and found something fascinating to stare at—a silk flower arrangement. He still remembered how she'd stared at him that first day he'd arrived at the camp, grimy from several days in the field, and how she'd watched openly while he showered, not bothering to hide her interest.

Still, they'd never ended up in bed together. She'd proved surprisingly prudish, once he'd gotten to know her. He understood why now—a princess simply didn't go sleeping around.

''Why don't I just move my things to another cabin?'' she suggested now.

''Because, no matter how careful we are, the crew will figure out we aren't sleeping together. And if word of that gets out, I'm in trouble.''

''No one in my mother's employ would dare breathe a word to the press.''

''Amelia, wake up. Someone on your mother's staff is doing just that. How else would Krissy Katwell be getting her information? Everyone has his price.''

''Hmm, good point. Okay, what do *you* suggest?''

He looked at the queen-size bed, then back at Amelia. ''There's plenty of room.''

She shook her head. ''That's not a good idea.''

''Relax, Princess,'' he said. ''I'm not after your virtue. I'll make up a pallet and sleep on the floor.''

''You can't. That would be so uncomfortable.''

''I'm used to it. I slept in a tree one time. It won't bother me a bit.''

''Okay, then. I'll just…get ready for bed.'' She grabbed her overnight case—the only luggage she'd brought, knowing there would be extra clothes on the *Duchess*—and slipped into the bathroom. He heard water running, then the weird sound of a marine toilet. When she emerged, he was surprised to see her wearing a pair of striped cotton jammies that would have looked at home on a nun.

"So sue me. These are comfortable."

He actually laughed.

"What were you expecting, a white negligee?"

He laughed even harder. "You are priceless, you know that? Who'd have thought Princess Amelia sleeps in men's cotton pajamas?"

"They're not men's. I got them from the Victoria's Secret catalog."

"They look like men's," he said as he took his turn in the head. When he came out, Amelia was under the covers up to her neck. She watched him almost suspiciously as he spread some blankets and a pillow on the carpeted floor. "You might want to turn out the lights now. I like to sleep comfortably, too— which does *not* involve pajamas."

The light went out before he'd finished the sentence.

DESPITE HER exhaustion, Amelia couldn't sleep. The events of the day kept rolling around in her brain, particularly her postwedding kiss to Nick. She'd expected to feel something. Their last kiss, at the Palemeir airport, had left her breathless and lightheaded. But she hadn't anticipated the barrage of fireworks that had assaulted her, or the hyperawareness of him that had carried on through the reception, the limo ride and up to this very moment.

She couldn't see him, but she could hear him

breathing a few feet away. And she knew he was naked.

Why hadn't she simply agreed to share the bed? Instead, she'd gone all virginal on him. Which made some sense, since she was a virgin. When one was a princess, one's movements were watched very closely. And those times she'd been living her alternate life as Melanie Lacey, she couldn't engage in any behavior that would reflect badly on the ICF or get her in hot water with them. The administrators never had been too crazy about including her on their relief missions because of the terrible press they would get should anything happen to her. Only her generous monetary donations had ensured her a role.

Anyway, she hadn't met anyone she'd really wanted to sleep with. Except Nick, but under the circumstances, a liaison had been impossible.

Now she had the right circumstances, and lots of time and privacy. They even had church approval. And she was making him sleep on the floor.

Well, what was she to do? If she seduced him, or jumped him, she'd be entering a level of intimacy she wasn't prepared for—and one that would be much harder to extract herself from when the six months was over.

So who says you can't make it real?

Even if Nick had been prepared to form a family with her and the kids when they married in Palemeir, that was before he'd known she was a member of the royal family.

Oh, who was she kidding? Even if Nick could stomach the thought of being married to a princess— for real—he would change his mind in a hurry once he learned she was going to be queen.

She better just not rock the boat. She would think of herself as the children's nanny for six months.

A hot-and-bothered nanny.

Pale peach light peeked through the curtains into the cabin. Dawn, and she'd hardly slept at all, while Mr. Coma on the floor over there obviously wasn't suffering the same pangs of doubt as she. She might as well get up and see what their travel plans were.

Nick was still sacked out when Amelia emerged from the head dressed in jeans and a sweater, one of the two outfits she'd hastily packed. There were lots of spare clothes in all sizes on board, so she wasn't too worried about running out of stuff to wear.

She first peeked into the children's bedroom. They slept soundly, which was no wonder to Amelia after the busy day they had yesterday.

She passed through the main salon and up a flight of stairs to the upper deck, where Captain Lammas and Dave were readying the boat for departure.

"Ah, good morning, Princess Amelia," Dave said when he spotted her. "Is everything on board to your liking?"

Amelia shivered in the early-morning cold. "Fine, thanks," she fibbed. "Where are we heading this morning?"

"Captain Lammas thought it would be a good idea to head south, where it's warmer. We'll miss the picturesque New England harbors like Martha's Vineyard and Newport, but at least we won't be freezin' our lips off. We might make it as far as Florida."

"That sounds fine. I'd just as soon stay away from the popular tourist spots, though. When we go ashore, we'll want to do so quietly." And even then, she wasn't sure how much anonymity they would be allowed. Hopefully the press hadn't yet learned of her and Nick's honeymoon plans, so people wouldn't be trying to spot them in every East Coast port from Maine to Florida. But she couldn't be sure.

"What sort of provisions have been made for meals?" she asked.

"Well, now, that's the rub," Dave said. "I understand Lady Charlotte tried to get a cook, but no one was available on such short notice. So I guess…I'll be fixing the meals. A galley full of groceries was delivered last night, so we won't starve."

"Dave, can you cook?"

"Frankly, no, Your Highness. But I can make a mean ham sandwich or heat up soup."

"You have other responsibilities. Why not let us take care of the meals?"

Dave looked horrified. "That wouldn't be proper, Princess."

"And stop calling me 'Your Highness' and 'Princess.' For this cruise, at least, I'm just Amelia, okay? And we'll manage the cooking." *We won't have much choice.*

"If that's what you really want. We'll be under way in about thirty minutes."

"In that case, I'll see what can be done about breakfast." She retreated through the hatch and down to the middle deck, where all of the guests' living and sleeping areas were located. The crew's accommodations were below, near the engine room and maintenance areas.

In the galley, Amelia opened the brushed-steel refrigerator to find it bulging with fruits and vegetables, fresh meats, eggs, milk and cheese, along with every sort of condiment one could desire. In the cabinets

kept cooking, getting blacker and blacker. She wasted precious time searching for a spatula, and more time just trying to maneuver the slippery strips of bacon onto the spatula and onto a plate.

That was when the smoke alarm went off.

Within thirty seconds, Dave and Jules rushed into the galley looking panicked. Dave immediately figured out the problem and did something to dismantle the smoke alarm, which was just outside the galley entrance.

"There's no fire," she said quickly. "I just let the bacon burn. I'm so sorry."

"Why don't you let me cook?" Jules asked.

"You can cook?"

"Well, I can heat up a can of soup."

Soup-heating seemed to be the skill of the day. "Then you're no better off than me. Maybe we should call the grocery store and have some TV dinners delivered."

Thunderous footsteps caught all of their attention, and Nick burst into the galley wearing gym shorts and nothing else. "What happened?"

"The smoke alarm went off," Amelia explained, though she had a hard time getting any words past her dry mouth. Her memories of Nick's almost naked body hadn't done him justice. He could have been a steel robot underneath all that taut, tanned skin.

"Don't tell me. You tried to cook."

"Mother wasn't able to hire a cook on short notice, so I thought I'd get breakfast started."

"And do us all a favor by burning the boat to a cinder?"

"I suppose you've never burned anything?"

"*I'll* get breakfast, okay?"

"Let me guess. You can heat up a can of soup."

Nick made a face. "Who would want soup for breakfast?"

"I just meant—"

"How do you think I feed the kids? We don't have McDonald's in my village. Now, would you like to clear out so I can get breakfast started?"

Amelia looked around and realized the other two men had escaped, not wanting to get involved in the royal couple's first marital tiff. She sincerely hoped none of them would be tempted to leak this story to Krissy Katwell.

"I don't believe I'm hungry anymore," she said. "But you go ahead."

Amelia withdrew and climbed up on deck. As the sun began to glimmer gold against Manhattan's sky-scrapers, she found a cushy deck chair to curl up in and sulk. So far, she was a complete failure as a wife.

Chapter Nine

When he was suddenly alone in the galley, Nick realized he was all but naked. Great. He must have made quite an impression on the staff.

He found a T-shirt, then checked on Josie and Jakob. "Uncle Nick?" Josie was just rousing, rubbing her eyes and looking around the room curiously. "Where are we?"

"On board a yacht."

"I know that. I was just wondering if we'd sailed anywhere yet."

"Not yet, but if you hurry and get dressed, you can watch us cast off and sail through New York Harbor."

"Then where are we going?"

"I don't know. Put on a sweater, it's cold outside. What do you want for breakfast?"

"Cornflakes," she said, the same request she made every morning.

"How about you, sleepyhead?" he said to Jakob, who was just waking up. "What sounds good for breakfast?"

"Pancakes!"

"Pancakes it is." The built-in griddle in the galley

would be perfect for pancakes in bulk. Once he scraped Amelia's burnt bacon off it, that is.

He was actually surprised that Amelia had even tried to fix breakfast. He was right about her ineptitude in the kitchen, but at least she'd made an attempt. He liked it that she didn't expect to be waited on hand and foot. But then, he'd already known that about her.

Unfortunately, his surprise, combined with being jolted out of a deep sleep, had caused him to be less than gracious toward her. He'd been in an aroused state due to a night filled with heated dreams about Amelia, so the abrupt wake-up call had made him doubly cranky. Maybe a plateful of fluffy pancakes would redeem him and bring her around. No one could resist his pancakes.

Twenty minutes later, with the kids' dubious help, Nick had two huge stacks of pancakes keeping warm in the oven. He even found some real maple syrup to put on them.

"Let's see who's hungry," he said, intending to go abovedecks and track down Amelia and the crew. Then he took a look at the children's footwear and realized slick-soled sandals would never do. "Better put on your tennis shoes first. Then we'll see about finding you some life jackets."

They ran back to their cabin to change shoes, and Nick went up on deck to see what was what. The boat was just pulling out of its berth, and the two crew members looked much too busy to think about breakfast. Jules, though, proclaimed himself to be ravenous.

That left Amelia.

"Have you seen my wife?" He startled himself by the use of that word, *wife*. He'd used it last night, to rankle Amelia, but he didn't think of her as his wife and wasn't likely to start.

Jules silently pointed toward the front of the boat. Nick made his way to the forward deck, where he found Amelia curled up in a deck chair wrapped up in an old jacket.

"Breakfast is ready."

She looked up, startled. Nick was once again struck by how truly beautiful Amelia was, with or without her princess trappings.

"I'm not hungry," she said.

"Are you embarrassed because you burned bacon?"

"No comment."

"Everybody burns bacon at some point in their lives."

"Yes, but I don't know the first thing about cooking. It was silly of me to try."

"As I recall, you cook up a mean pot of beans and rice."

"That's the extent of my culinary skills. Otherwise, I was taught to manage a household staff."

He'd guessed as much about her. "So what? I'll teach you to cook, if you want."

"Would you really?" She actually sounded eager.

"We've got six months to kill."

"It's not just the cooking, you know. It occurs to me I'm not very well equipped to function in the real world."

"What are you talking about? You don't think Palemeir was the real world?"

"Not in the way I mean. When I'm on a relief mission, I'm under the protection and authority of the ICF. I don't make decisions, I just do what I'm told.

I've never even kept a checkbook, or gone to a grocery store. Everything's always been done for me.''

"Hmm, I see the dilemma. Is that why you're reluctant to go to Montavi? We could hire someone to help out—''

"No, no, I don't want you to hire me a servant. Heavens, I've had enough of that. I was just wondering…how I can be an effective…I need to know more about how normal, middle-class people live, but I don't believe that will ever be possible.''

"Sure it is. Anytime you want, we can go to Montavi. You can shop at the marketplace and cook and do laundry to your heart's content. But I don't think it will compare to life on a luxury yacht.''

"It sounds wonderful. But how could I do all that? I don't exactly blend in.''

"You mean because you're the king's granddaughter? No one will care too much in Montavi. Oh, there might be a flurry of curiosity seekers at first, but it'll be old news in a few days and they'll leave you alone.''

"I wish that was true. Nick, there's something I haven't told you. I'm not supposed to tell anyone, actually, but since you're married to me, that makes you a member of the royal family, at least temporarily, and you have a right to know.''

"Know what?''

Little footsteps tromping toward them halted the conversation. Josie and Jakob, nearly swallowed up by their orange life jackets, burst onto the forward deck with Dave ushering them along.

"You've got a couple of hungry mates, here,'' Dave said in his best pirate imitation.

"I'm the second mate,'' Josie said, "and Jakob's

the third mate. Dave said so. I guess you two can be fourth and fifth mates."

"Oh, no, I'm nothing so honorable," Nick said. "I'm the galley slave."

"And what about Auntie Mellie?"

"She's the head honcho," Nick said. "She gets to boss everybody around."

"That's right," Josie said with great authority. "She's a princess, so she can do anything."

"I think on a boat, the captain is still the head guy," Amelia said. "Even over a princess."

"Shoot," Josie said. "I thought maybe you could make the captain sail us to someplace far away like Africa or New Jersey, and we could stay on this boat forever."

"You like the boat?" Amelia asked.

"Uh-huh. I'm not seasick or anything."

Of course, they'd only inched a few hundred feet away from the dock.

"Two weeks will seem like forever, trust me," Nick said. "Now, let's go see about breakfast." He offered Amelia a hand up, and she reluctantly took it.

Everyone enjoyed the pancakes, even Josie, who'd been persuaded to try them after she discovered that, horror of horrors, no cornflakes were aboard, only granola and Rice Krispies. Dave gobbled his down, then relieved Captain Lammas so he could have breakfast.

Amelia, though, was pensive, and Nick wondered what she'd been about to tell him before the children had interrupted them. Her concerns about her ivory-tower status as a princess amused him. She was definitely a puzzle, equally at home in a satin dress sipping champagne or in camouflage fatigues chewing on a piece of beef jerky for dinner. It was the middle ground that confounded her.

He hoped there would be no more talk of cutting the cruise short. He looked forward to getting to know his bride in a whole new way. If they'd only planned on a couple of weeks as a married couple, he could have easily given up on the idea of making love to Amelia. But six months living with this exquisite woman and not taking her to bed? That was insanity. Even Monette would not expect him to be a monk.

Of course, he'd set himself up for failure by making it sound as if it would be six months of torture, as she'd so ably pointed out. He had his work cut out for him.

THE NEXT FEW DAYS went far more smoothly than Amelia could have predicted.

The children stayed in good spirits, finding all kinds of things to entertain them, from bird-watching to videotapes to storybooks, which Josie took it upon herself to read aloud to Jakob in an effort to improve her reading.

But far more interesting to Amelia was Nick's attitude, which seemed to have shifted gently. He showed her how to cook a few simple meals, much to her delight. They pitched in together to keep the boat clean. Nick showed her how to run the washer and dryer, the vacuum, the dishwasher, and none of these tasks proved difficult. Hester and other members of the Carradigne staff had been using household appliances in front of her her whole life; she'd just never paid attention before.

As the *Duchess* moved farther south, the weather warmed, and they all shed their sweaters and pants for shorts and swimsuits. Captain Lammas docked the boat in a deserted cove off South Carolina, where they all indulged in a private swim. The water was still a bit chilly, but the children didn't seem to even notice. Nick showed particular delight in showing Josie how to dive for shells on the sandy bottom.

Amelia herself wasn't a strong swimmer, but she could float on her back for hours on end. This she did, earning a slight sunburn despite the sunblock she'd applied. They had a wienie roast on the beach, then reboarded the boat and set off once again.

"I could get used to this kind of life," Amelia confessed as she leaned on the railing near the bow, watching the spectacular fiery sunset. "I've always abhorred the idea of being one of the idle rich. That was why I started working for the ICF. But all this lazy self-indulgence is kind of nice. I mean, have you ever seen such a sunset?"

"Red sky at night, sailor's delight," Nick said. He stood next to her, watching the scenery with one eye and the kids with another. Jakob and Josie were playing with some toy trucks on deck, watching them roll back and forth with the pitch of the boat, which was more pronounced this evening than it had been since they'd left port. Jules, who had little to occupy his time, was watching the kids, too, so they were well chaperoned.

"I guess that means we don't have to worry about storms," Amelia said.

"I wouldn't put your money on that prediction. Dave said we'll be dodging a few squalls tonight."

The thought of bad weather made Amelia slightly queasy. She was sure her mother wouldn't hire a boat captain who was anything but first-rate, but in chatting with Captain Lammas, she'd learned that this was only his third stint in charge of the *Duchess*. Still, his twenty-plus years of seafaring experience put her mind at ease—for the most part.

"Maybe we ought to get dinner started, in case it gets too rough to cook." The words to "The Wreck of the *Edmund Fitzgerald*" came to her mind without effort, about how the seas had been too rough to fix dinner. That was right before the boat sank.

"It's all but done. I put a stew on this morning before we dropped anchor at the cove. Should be ready whenever anyone's hungry."

"Shall I make rolls to go with the stew?" She felt very proud, making that offer. Nick had taught her to make light-as-air rolls the previous day.

"Sure, why not?"

They left Jules to watch the kids and went below to the galley. As she sifted flour and baking powder, then added the other ingredients to the dough, Amelia noticed the movement of the boat more than she had in the past. Several times she lost her footing and had to grab onto the counter to stop herself from toppling over.

"You've got flour on your nose, Princess."

Amelia didn't mind anymore when Nick called her "Princess." She'd started to think of it as a form of endearment. And she did, in fact, have flour on her nose, which she could plainly see in the glass oven door. She grabbed a dish towel and swiped at it.

"Better?" She turned toward Nick for his inspection.

Just then the boat made a particularly violent lurch, and she fell right into him.

He took one step back to absorb her weight and

stay on his own feet. Then he steadied her by grasping her shoulders and setting her aright. But instead of releasing her, his arms slid around her.

"Let me just have a closer look at that nose." He peered down at her critically while her heart tried to thump its way out of her chest. She could have sworn he was looking at her as if he wanted to kiss her. "No, I don't believe you got it all," he said as he brushed at something on the side of her nose, then her cheek. Then his hand slid down to cup her jaw, and she knew she was right.

Recalling the lousy job she'd done on their kiss at the wedding, she determined to make up for it with this one. Instead of waiting for him to kiss her, she stood up on her toes and met him halfway.

It was a tiny slice of heaven, his lips joining hers, their breath mingling, bodies pressing close. It made her feel wild and reckless and just a little bit naughty, even though they were married. Imagine, feeling guilty for kissing your own husband....

Then the boat lurched again, hurling them apart with the same force it had brought them together.

Nick laughed. "We're at the mercy of the waves."

"So it seems."

Amelia heard the main hatch open and the unmistakable sound of children clamoring down the stairs. "Uncle Nick?" came Josie's plaintive voice before she even made it to the galley. "Uncle Nick, Jules said we have to come downstairs because it's too rough. Can't we stay up on deck a little longer? It's not raining or anything, just a little ocean spray."

When Josie, Jakob and Jules entered the galley, Amelia could see they were damp. The weather must have worsened, because the spray hadn't been washing over the deck a few minutes earlier.

"I think you better listen to Jules," Nick said. "The ocean is tricky. A big wave could wash up on deck and take you out to sea, and we might not even notice you were gone." Nick meant to tease, but Josie took this discussion very seriously.

"I'll hold on to the railing," she said. "I want to watch the storm. It's the most coolest thing I've ever seen."

"You can watch it out those big windows in the saloon," Nick suggested.

"It's not the same!" Josie objected. "You're not being fair!"

This was the first time Amelia had seen Josie act like a brat. It was probably a good sign. Before, she'd been too afraid of the consequences to defy authority.

"Don't talk back to me, please, Josie," Nick said wearily. "It might not be fair, but I'm the parent, so I get to make the rules."

"You're not my father," Josie said, near tears. "The adoption isn't real. Why don't you just send me to the orphanage?" With that, she ran toward her cabin in the full throes of a seven-year-old's tantrum.

Nick sighed. "She overhears a lot more than I think she does."

"I'm sure she'll be fine," Jules said. "She's overtired. I have a girl just a couple of years older, so I've been through this."

Amelia knew Josie, with her quicksilver moods, would recover quickly. She wasn't so sure about the weather. "Jules, how bad is the storm?"

"Bad enough, I guess. Dave has started lashing down everything on—"

The boat made another dramatic sway.

"—excuse me." Jules lunged toward the bathroom.

Nick exchanged a worried look with Amelia. "I'll go check it out. You watch the rolls. Jakob, you help Auntie Mellie with dinner."

Jakob didn't seem to care that he'd been pulled belowdecks. He delighted in babbling to Amelia as she straightened up the galley and kept an eye on the baking rolls.

Amelia was just pulling the rolls from the oven when Nick returned. "What did Captain Lammas say?"

"I didn't talk to him. He looked far too busy checking radar and charts and listening to weather reports. But I talked to Dave. He said it's nothing to worry about, just a routine line of squalls. He's been through lots of storms, and so has the captain. And this is a very seaworthy boat."

Nick didn't sound entirely convinced of the argument as reported.

"Is there anything we should do?"

"Eat dinner while we can still keep the stew in the bowls. And we should stow away anything we don't want to bounce around."

It was a small party around the dinner table that evening. Captain Lammas and Dave were too busy to eat. Jules was too ill, and Josie too busy sulking. Nick could have ordered Josie to the table, but he didn't have the heart for it. "She's testing her boundaries, I think," Nick said.

"It's okay. You won the important battle. Whether she eats dinner isn't all that crucial. The less attention we pay her while she's sulking, the better."

So it was just the two of them and Jakob, who ate hungrily, imitating Nick gesture for gesture.

Amelia didn't have much appetite herself.

After they ate, she put some of the stew into two plastic cups, along with two plastic-wrapped rolls, and took them up to the crew. She put the cups of stew into cup holders on the bridge and wedged the bread in a crevice where it wouldn't roll away. Captain Lammas gave her an absent nod. It was raining now, and Amelia could hardly keep her footing as she made her way down the hatch.

They spent the evening watching out the windows, for what good it did them. Visibility was nil. Every once in a while, lightning illuminated the ocean surface, and they could make out waves that looked big enough to swamp the boat. Josie eventually came out of her cabin to watch with everyone else, saying little. But she did end up crawling into Nick's lap.

For the children's sake, Amelia tried to put an optimistic spin on the storm, pointing out how powerful and beautiful nature was, and how this was an adventure they could tell their own children someday. But after they managed to put the kids to bed, lashing them into their bunks with safety straps, Amelia dropped her guard.

"Frankly, I'm just a little bit scared," she said to Nick. "Aren't you?"

"I'm not thrilled. But I'm sure the captain knows what he's doing. This is a big boat. It would take a helluva storm to sink it."

"You don't think this *is* a helluva storm?"

"I was in a typhoon once in India. Compared to that, this is a cakewalk."

"If you say so."

"Let's turn in. By morning it'll be over."

A few minutes later, Amelia sat cross-legged on the bed, safely garbed in her pajamas, while Nick, still fully dressed, sat in a chair leafing through a book of old nautical charts.

"I'm not sleepy," she announced.

"Neither am I."

"I feel like we ought to be *doing* something. Are you sure the captain doesn't need our help? I mean, I could listen to the radio or something."

"We'd only be a hindrance on deck or on the bridge."

"I just can't get my mind off the *Edmund Fitzgerald.*"

"The what?"

"You know, that ship on the Great Lakes that sank in a storm and drowned everyone on board. Gordon Lightfoot did a song about it. It's really creepy."

"We're not going to sink."

A clap of thunder shook the whole boat, and Amelia's heart jumped into her throat. "I just wish I could think about something else."

Nick looked up and gave her a mischievous grin. "You need a distraction."

"A rousing game of backgammon isn't going to do it."

"Backgammon was the furthest thing from my mind. In fact, I was thinking about that kiss in the galley. So rudely interrupted..."

Amelia felt her face heating. She'd been trying *not* to think about that kiss, and with the storm raging all around, she'd managed to push it to the back of her mind. But now, here it was in the forefront again, causing a storm to brew inside her, matching the one outside.

Nick put aside his book and moved from the chair to the bed, lounging next to her as if he did it every day. "I bet I could make you forget all about the storm."

He wouldn't get any takers, not in this room. "Um," was all she could think of to say.

"I've been fantasizing about what you look like under those manly pajamas."

"What...what about...I thought we had a business arrangement."

"It's still a business arrangement, if you prefer to think of it that way," Nick said smoothly. "But we'll be in business for six months. There's no way I can share a room with you for that long and not...take a look at the books." Nick gave a mischievous grin.

Amelia's mouth felt as though it was full of cotton while the rest of her was awash with longing. It would be so easy to accept what he offered, no strings attached. Throw herself into intimacy, consequences be damned. But there would be consequences, unpleasant ones. Although she'd never been in a serious romantic relationship, she'd read things and heard them from her friends. She'd seen firsthand the torture CeCe had gone through when she'd fallen in love with Shane but believed he didn't return her feelings.

Making love with Nick would simply make it all that much easier to *fall in* love with him. And should that happen, she would not be in an enviable position.

Nick stroked her hand lightly, his caress a question. She drew back.

"I don't think this is a good idea."

"May I ask why not? We're married."

"We might be married in the eyes of our respective governments, but you know as well as I do that a true marriage requires commitment—and *that* we don't have."

Nick's teasing smile faded.

"It's not a matter of prudishness on my part," she continued. "A man can have sex and then go watch a football game without giving it a second thought. Women aren't built that way. If I…with you, it would change me. I don't want to be changed in that way."

She could tell he really didn't understand what she was saying, but that was as much explanation as she was prepared to give. She couldn't come out and tell him she was afraid of falling in love with him, when she knew that love was something he couldn't give her in return.

Nick rolled over on his side, facing away from her. "Does this mean I have to keep sleeping on the floor?"

"You mean this whole seduction thing was to get you off the floor? If that's your only problem, you can have the bed. *I'll* sleep on the floor."

"Believe me, that was not my only—" The boat gave a particularly violent lurch, and Nick rolled off onto the carpet.

Amelia would have laughed if she hadn't been so afraid. "Nick, this isn't normal. I thought we would be skirting the squalls."

He sat up, rubbing his elbow where he'd apparently bumped it in the fall. "I'm sure the captain would let us know if there were any real problems."

On cue, someone knocked at the cabin door. Amelia and Nick exchanged a look; Amelia answered the door to find Dave standing there.

"What's wrong?" she asked.

"This may sound like a strange question," Dave said, looking at Nick, "but did you put any saffron in the stew?"

"The yellow stuff? Yeah. Why?"

"It seems Captain Lammas is deathly allergic to saffron."

"Is he all right?" Amelia asked, alarmed.

"He took an antihistamine injection, and he informs me he'll live. But he's in no condition to pilot this boat. And Jules is still heaving in his cabin. Begging your pardon, Your Highness," he added with an apologetic nod toward Amelia.

Nick was already pushing his feet into deck shoes. "Just tell me what to do."

"I'll need both of you. The satellite positioning system has been knocked out of whack, so Nick, I'd like you at the bow, keeping an eye out for buoys, rocks, other boats—anything that might get in our way. Princess Amelia, I'd like you to monitor the sonar and man the radio. I want everyone in life jackets, too."

Dave turned and headed out, fully expecting his makeshift crew to follow orders.

Nick and Amelia looked at each other again. Nick said nothing, but Amelia was sure he was thinking the same thing she was—the storm was no longer a minor inconvenience, but a life-threatening disaster.

Chapter Ten

Amelia didn't even bother dressing, just put on her shoes. She and Nick paused only long enough to wrestle the drowsy children into their life jackets and strap them back into their bunks. Fortunately, neither seemed to be scared, which was a little sad to Amelia. They'd been through explosions and gunfire and depravations and had watched both of their parents die. A little storm at sea was nothing to them.

She and Nick donned rain gear and life jackets, then went on deck, where they were immediately soaked to the skin by sheets of driving rain that gusted up under their jackets and inside their sleeves and collars.

Dave handed Nick a safety harness and showed him how to connect to a jack line, which would prevent him from being washed overboard. The two men would stay connected via walkie-talkie. On the bridge, Nick instructed Amelia on how to read the sonar and to warn them if the boat was heading into shallow water. She was also to listen to the radio for weather reports and reports from other boats, and be prepared to issue a May Day message on the off chance things got any dicier.

They held their own for a while. Dave headed the yacht into the waves at a forty-five-degree angle, powering down the engines so that they were almost stationary.

"Shouldn't we try to make it into some port?" Amelia asked.

"We're too far from any shelter, and the slower we go, the less strain the waves put on the hull and superstructure. As it is, I need to check the bilge, probably pump it out, and make sure all the windows and ports are holding up. Can you take the helm for a few minutes?"

"Me?" Amelia squeaked.

"There's nothing to it. You've been watching me. Just head her straight into the waves to keep her from rolling sideways."

Amelia took the wheel with no small amount of trepidation, feeling the weight of the six lives that were now in her hands. But she soon found she had an instinct for making the small corrections necessary to navigate straight through the waves. She couldn't imagine what Nick was going through. All she saw of him was a flash of his yellow slicker now and then, reassuring her he was still on deck. But she couldn't imagine how he stayed there, the way the waves were washing over the bow.

When Dave reappeared a few minutes later, his face was a bloodless white. "One of the portholes broke out, in the Blue Cabin."

"Oh my God. The children!"

"Jakob is in the saloon. He's frightened, but he's fine. I could not find Josie. I'm going to look for her now."

Amelia froze, her clammy skin suddenly like ice.

Josie had wanted to go on deck, and Nick wouldn't let her. Her outwardly polite and soft-spoken nature hid a streak of willfulness, especially when Nick gave orders.

"I'll find her," she said, turning the wheel back to Dave.

"Put on a harness if you're going out on deck."

Though it took precious seconds, Amelia followed Dave's instructions. Getting herself washed overboard wouldn't help matters.

She checked the aft deck first, calling Josie's name, even though her voice would be hard to hear in the storm, and searching for a bright orange life jacket. She caught a glimpse of a bright orange spot halfway down the deck and sighed with relief, rushing to grab the little girl and whisk her to safety—except—it was just a coil of rope.

She dreaded having to tell Nick his child was missing, but when an initial search failed to turn up Josie, Amelia made her way on the fiercely rocking deck to the bow. Because the wind was howling, he couldn't hear her call his name. She grabbed his arm. He whirled around, almost striking her, then looked at her with a mixture of relief and anxiety.

"Josie's missing," she said simply.

She'd never seen such stark terror on a man's face, but he quickly regained his poise and took control of the situation. "Did you tell Dave?"

"Yes. The boat is all but stopped."

"Take the port side, I'll take the starboard. Search the deck and the water, working your way to the back of the boat. Are you sure she's not below somewhere?"

"No. We haven't made a thorough search. But I

didn't want to waste time with that if she's out here somewhere."

"Good thinking."

"Nick—look!" Amelia had glimpsed a flash of orange in the water, probably a hundred feet from the boat. By the time Nick peered out in the direction she indicated, the view again held nothing but gray water and gray rain. "I saw something, I know I did."

"Stay here. Keep pointing in the direction where you saw it." He took out the walkie-talkie and asked Dave to turn to starboard.

"There, I saw it again. It's her, Nick, I know it is."

"Keep pointing. Did you copy, Dave? We see her. A hundred feet starboard, straight out." While he talked, Nick attached a lifeline to his safety harness, then checked to see that the length was sufficient. "Take the slack out of this line as it's needed. I'm going in."

"Wait until we're closer—" But her words fell on deaf ears. He handed her the walkie-talkie, climbed up on the railing and jumped into the water, not even wasting the small amount of time it would take to climb down the ladder. He briefly submerged, and Amelia held on to the railing to keep from collapsing with worry. He jumped a long way—he could have injured himself. But soon he reappeared and started swimming toward where they'd seen Josie's life jacket.

Huge waves washed over him again and again, but each time he surfaced, never breaking stride. Amelia marveled at his strength and determination even as she agonized over the outcome of his rescue mission.

It seemed to take hours, but as the boat turned, drawing slowly nearer to Josie, Nick gained ground—

or rather, water. The two scraps of orange grew closer, until finally they merged. Amelia drew a relieved breath. They weren't out of danger yet, but at least Nick and Josie were together.

She started reeling them in, taking up the slack as the boat closed the distance between it and Nick and Josie. The yacht pitched crazily as the waves hit it from the side instead of straight on, and twice Amelia thought she would join Nick and Josie in the water. But she always managed to grab onto something in time to keep from being washed overboard.

She got on the walkie-talkie. "Dave, they're almost at the boat. How do we get them back on board?" It seemed that if the boat didn't maneuver just right, it could crash right into Nick and Josie, landing on top of them.

"I'll cut the engines so there's no danger from the propellers. Signal them to the stern, and I'll lower a ladder."

Amelia waved wildly to Nick and pointed toward the back of the boat. At first he didn't seem to get it, but then he changed direction. In the rough water, and dragging Josie with him, he made scant progress, but minute by agonizing minute he drew closer. Finally she could make out his face through the rain, which seemed to be letting up a bit. She could also see that Josie was conscious, struggling against Nick in a panic. That was a good sign. They were both going to make it.

Dave came to help her, and she heaved on the line with all her strength, making sure Nick didn't lose any of the progress he'd made, doing her part to drag him to the right spot.

At last Nick's hand made contact with the ladder.

He paused there, resting, gasping for air. Josie seemed to calm down a bit, and he shifted her to one side so he could climb up, one weary rung at a time. When he reached the top, he handed Josie wordlessly to Amelia and Dave.

Amelia put her arms around the shivering child. "Oh, Josie, baby, are you okay? Are you hurt?"

Josie said nothing, but her thin arms snaked their way around Amelia's neck.

Dave offered a hand to Nick. "You better both get below and get warm. Hypothermia's a real risk, especially for a tiny thing like Josie."

Nick looked as if he wanted to take Josie back and hold her safe from nature's violence, but he also looked as if he'd spent every last ounce of strength getting her back on board.

"I've got her," Amelia said, in awe of what she'd just witnessed. She'd known he was a hero—King Easton had said Nick had performed all sorts of brave acts in the military and as an independent soldier. She'd believed the king, of course, but seeing Nick's heroism firsthand made it more immediate, more real.

Below, Amelia turned the thermostat up to eighty-five degrees first thing, then found blankets in a linen closet and instructed Nick to take off all his clothes. Unquestionably he'd been in charge of the rescue, but the ICF had trained her in first aid and she knew all about hypothermia. She immediately set about removing Josie's soggy life jacket and clothes. The girl wasn't wearing shoes or socks, and Amelia wondered if the force of the waves had sucked them right off her feet. But what worried her more was Josie's listlessness, and her slightly blue-tinged lips.

Jakob watched intently as Amelia dried Josie's thin

little body, rubbing briskly with a towel, then wrapped her in two blankets and held her close, hoping to infuse some of her own body heat to Josie.

"Will she die and go to heaven with Mama and Papa?" Jakob asked worriedly.

"Oh, sweetheart, no, of course not. Your sister's fine, just cold." She spared Jakob a quick hug before returning to Josie's care, thinking it ought to be Nick reassuring Jakob. But so far he'd said nothing. He was just standing there, dripping on the carpet. "Nick, hadn't you better change clothes?"

"Are you sure she'll be all right?" Nick asked, his voice hoarse.

"I'm no doctor, but I think she'll be fine." Amelia pressed her ear to Josie's chest. "She's breathing okay. I don't hear anything sloshing around in there. Right now, she just needs to warm up. And so do you," she said pointedly. "You're not immune from a chill, you know."

"You're not exactly dry yourself."

"I'm not shivering. Nick, for once will you just do what you're told? You won't be any help to the children if you catch pneumonia."

"Pneumonia," Jakob said, testing the word. He'd heard it before, she realized. That was what his mother had died from. But surely he'd been too young to remember that.

Nick still didn't move. He just stared at Josie, as if willing her to recover. And sure enough, in a few minutes, she did. Her color returned to normal, and she began wiggling restively in her blanket cocoon.

"I'm hot."

"How about we go find you a clean nightgown."

She nodded. "Uncle Nick?"

"Yes, Josie."

"I almost drowned."

"I'm aware of that."

"You saved my life, didn't you?"

"Yes. You almost got us both killed by disobeying me."

"But the—"

"I don't want to hear any excuses."

Amelia cringed. *Nick, not now.* The poor child did not need a lecture. She needed love and reassurance from her father. Tomorrow should be soon enough to talk about rules and why it's important to follow them.

Josie buried her face against Amelia's shoulder, and Amelia gave Nick a hard look. "I'll put the kids back to bed."

He headed to the main cabin without another word, leaving wet carpet in his wake.

As soon as Amelia opened the door to the Blue Cabin, she understood the severity of the porthole giving way. The whole room was flooded. Water must have rushed into the cabin like a fire hose.

"I just wanted to tell someone there was a flood," Josie said on a sob. "I didn't disobey on purpose."

"It's all right, sweetheart. Uncle Nick will understand when he calms down and you explain it to him. He's not really mad at you. It's just that almost losing you frightened him. Sometimes men don't like for people to know they're scared, so they hide it by acting mad."

"Uncle Nick must be scared a lot, then."

Out of the mouths of babes.

"Well, it's a cinch you can't sleep in here tonight. Let's try one of the other cabins." She quickly found another empty cabin, a luxurious room with a double bed. "Looks like you'll have to share."

"That's okay," Josie said. "Jakob and I used to sleep in the same bed all the time. He was littler then."

"Would you rather sleep in our cabin?" Amelia asked. It occurred to her that the kids, having just gone through such an ordeal, might not want to be alone.

Josie seemed to struggle with her answer. "No," she finally said. "We'll be okay, won't we, Jakob?"

Jakob nodded. He hadn't taken his eyes off his sister since Amelia had brought her downstairs.

Amelia didn't blame Josie for wanting to avoid Nick at the moment. Tomorrow would be soon enough for them to reconcile. "If you get scared or you just want a hug, you know where to find me, right?"

Both children nodded. Jakob looked anxiously at the porthole.

"The storm's letting up now," Amelia said, trying to reassure him with a smile. "This cabin will stay dry."

She kissed them both, and this time Josie accepted the show of affection and returned it in kind. Amelia's heart contracted. Suddenly she felt like a mother, which was both wonderful and painful. Painful because she knew these children weren't hers to keep. But she wouldn't withhold anything from them, despite Nick's misgivings. For the next six months, she was laying claim to them.

She went on deck to report to Dave, and found the bridge far calmer. Jules was there, looking a bit pale but otherwise all right.

"We've moved through the worst of it now," Dave said. "How's Josie?"

"She'll be fine. I put her to bed. We need to do something about the Blue Cabin."

"I'll take care of it," Jules said. "I seem to have found my sea legs."

"Dave, what do you need me to do?" Amelia asked.

"Everything's under control. Get warm and dry yourself. If you catch even a cold, Lady Charlotte won't be pleased with me."

Amelia took him at his word. She was exhausted and shivering.

When she entered her own cabin, she expected to hear the shower running in the bathroom. Instead, she found Nick sitting on the floor, leaning against the wall with the comforter from the bed wrapped around him.

"Nick!" Oh my God, she thought, what if *he* was the one suffering from hypothermia?

"How's she doing?" Nick's voice was not as strong and sure as it normally was.

"She's fine." Amelia peeled the damp bedspread away from his body. He still wore his life jacket and rain gear. She felt an urge to lecture him, but realized that, like Josie, he didn't need scolding. Obviously he simply hadn't had one ounce of energy left, or he would have taken better care of himself.

Wordlessly she unzipped the life jacket and lifted it over his head. The rain slicker came next. He didn't protest as she unbuttoned his sopping polo shirt and pulled it off.

She'd never been quite this close to his bare chest before, but she tried not to think about how it affected her. She was in caregiving mode, not seduction mode. She had to get Nick warm and dry.

He was trembling.

"I think we should get you into the shower," she said, touching the bare skin of his shoulder. She expected to find it freezing, but he was actually warm. Then it hit her. He wasn't trembling from cold, but from the aftereffects of almost losing Josie.

Amelia didn't think about what she did next. She just put her arms around Nick and held him. She wondered how long it had been since anyone had comforted this man. He was used to being the one in charge, the one who came to the rescue and helped everyone else.

Perhaps that was why he'd been so distant with her since she'd offered to marry him. He didn't like being on the receiving end of comfort.

For several long seconds he didn't accept her hugging him, but neither did he push her away. He sat straight and stiff, enduring the embrace. But she didn't give up, and after a few more seconds, he gradually softened, and his arms went around her, drawing in her softness and warmth.

"I don't know what I would have done if I'd lost her," he said in a hoarse voice.

"But you didn't, so don't even think about it."

"Thank you for what you did. I couldn't have rescued her alone."

"You know I'd do anything for those children."

"Maybe I should go help Dave."

"You're not going anywhere but to bed. Anyway, the storm's passed, and Jules is on his feet again."

"I should talk to Josie. I didn't mean to yell at her."

"I explained to her that you weren't mad, just frightened out of your wits. She's asleep now, I'm sure. Talk to her in the morning."

He made no move to release Amelia. In fact, as they'd talked, she'd somehow wound up sitting in his lap. Her own pajamas weren't exactly dry, and she savored the warmth of their entwined bodies.

At some point she became distinctly aware of a change in mood. First it was Nick, moving one hand to stroke her jaw. Then she found her face buried against his hair and a pool of heat building deep at her core. Finally, she could not miss the fact that her husband was aroused.

Amelia felt no need to remove herself. Earlier, when Nick had attempted his somewhat bloodless seduction, she'd been tempted, but also thoroughly convinced she should resist. But the events of the past hour or so had irrevocably changed things between them. Their shared concern over Josie had strengthened the fragile bond between them.

Maybe that was all they would ever have—a shared concern for the children. But for now, it was enough.

Amelia had only to turn her head slightly to bring her mouth to Nick's. In a heartbeat they'd sunk into a deep, soulful kiss. This was the passion she remembered of the Nicholas Standish she'd met in Palemeir. This was the airport kiss—only better, because it wasn't a kiss goodbye. It was more like a homecoming.

Like a flower greedy for sunlight, Amelia welcomed Nick's rising passion. His kisses grew hungrier, more intense, his tongue ravishing her mouth, pushing past teeth that were only minutes ago chattering with fear.

Nick pushed her onto her back on the thick carpet. With his hands on her shoulders, pinning her down, he kissed her with a thoroughness that was beyond Amelia's comprehension. She was inexperienced when it came to physical intimacy, but if a kiss could awaken her body like this, what must the rest of love-making be like?

She tentatively explored his back with her palms, and with each light stroke, Nick tensed and groaned. Her power to evoke such a strong response with such a small gesture emboldened her. She did not want him to realize how ignorant she was. So she pushed her hands between their bodies and reached for his shorts. She had the top button unfastened before he realized what she was about and pulled away, rolling to the carpet beside her.

He breathed heavily, almost gasping.

"Nick?" Had she done something wrong? She didn't want to be some passive rag doll, but maybe he didn't like aggressive women.

"Just give me a moment." He squeezed his eyes shut, as if he was in pain.

Amelia sat up and unfastened her pajama top. She would leave no room for doubt in Nick's head about what she wanted. He was the one who said they couldn't live together for six months without giving in to temptation, and at the moment she quite agreed. A marble statue couldn't sleep in the same room with him, night after night, and not go a little crazy with lust.

She'd had no idea such wantonness lurked beneath her skin. In moments she had the pajama top off, wadded up and tossed into a corner, despite the fact she'd never dropped clothes on the floor in her life.

She wiggled out of her bottoms next, along with her panties, relieved to have the damp clothes away from her skin.

When Nick opened his eyes, he found her kneeling naked beside him. His eyes widened in surprise. "Mellie."

His use of the old nickname warmed her. A show of fondness, he'd said of his use of the name that first day he'd come to the penthouse. Fondness wasn't love, but it was as much as Amelia needed right now.

He pulled her down beside him and resumed conquering her body, one square inch at a time. He stroked her belly, then her thighs, all the while kissing her, alternating tender assaults with breath-halting, almost savage kisses. His exploring hands deliberately avoided her breasts, and the more sensitive areas between her thighs, until she literally ached for him to touch her there.

He paused long enough to take off the rest of his clothes, accomplishing the task in a heated fit. She tried not to stare at his manhood, but perhaps this was not the time to be polite. Anyway, she was riveted. She had seen naked men before, in war zone hospitals, bathing in rivers, and once she'd witnessed an African tribal dance that involved lots of nudity. But she'd never seen quite such a stunning display of naked virility.

"You're protected?" he asked.

"What?" The question brought her back to her senses, and she was stunned she hadn't thought of something so basic as birth control. "No."

"No?" He grew very still.

Amelia thought the wonderful closeness they'd found was going to end tragically, until she remembered Lucia's ever-so-thoughtful gift. "Don't move." She pushed herself up and went to her overnight case. Moments later she returned to Nick with a handful of plastic packets in neon colors. "Will these do?"

"So *that's* what Lucia gave you as you got into the limo."

"How did you know that?"

"Lucky guess." He pulled her against him, then dragged her onto the bed.

Though Amelia seemed ready for the main event, Nick was in no rush. A few minutes earlier he'd been in danger of losing control. But with some slow breathing, he'd managed to rein in his fevered libido—he was not going to bed Amelia like some randy teenager. He imagined she'd had some sophisticated lovers, and, male animal that he was, he didn't want her making unfavorable comparisons.

Besides, he wanted to spend some time and attention on her breasts. They were full and firm and ripe, and at his first touch, he knew for a fact they were all-natural.

He stroked both nipples with his thumbs, feeling them harden beneath his touch. She gasped when he placed his mouth on one and suckled.

"It's too much," she whispered. "Please."

No such thing as too much. He touched the crop of gold curls that protected her femininity, and she rewarded him with another gasp. As he continued to kiss her breast, she urged her thighs open. She was too tense. He wanted her to relax.

The moment he pressed his fingers against her sensitive folds, she cried out. Nick couldn't believe it. He'd hardly begun, and he'd brought her to climax. Her responsiveness excited him beyond belief.

"Oh," she said. "Oh. S-sorry, that was a bit un-expected."

Leave it to the princess to be polite during sex. He slid up to kiss her lips again, and brought her arms around his neck. He applied himself diligently, and soon she was writhing beneath him again, making soft little moaning noises in the back of her throat.

He was pretty worked up himself. He grabbed a neon-pink packet, which had spilled over the blanket, and ripped it open with his teeth. He extracted the contents and handed it to her.

She gave him a look that said she was clueless. Well, hell, maybe Her Highness had never been required to do physical labor in bed. He took back the sheath and did the honors himself.

Moments later he was poised to enter her, savoring that delicious moment of anticipation. He'd fantasized about this far more often than he wanted to admit, even to himself. He'd wanted to be immune to her, to discipline his mind just as he disciplined his body, but that had proved impossible.

He entered as slowly as he could, enjoying the tight fit. But there came a point when he realized she was more than just tight. "Amelia?"

"Just do it," she pleaded.

He couldn't. She was a... He'd never in his life... Why hadn't she told...

She lifted her hips in invitation. The slight change of angle did something to him. Prompted by slight insanity, he plunged inside her, all the while thinking, *I'm deflowering a princess.* King Easton might behead him for that.

Then he remembered they were married, and his panic eased. "Amelia?" he said again.

She smiled up at him, though her eyes shone with tears. "That wasn't so bad." She wiggled beneath him, perhaps trying to get more comfortable, and her movements drove him to distraction. He could not hold himself in check much longer.

Out of consideration for her, he moved slowly, keeping a close eye on her face for any distress. After the sweet way she'd given herself to him, even knowing they had no future, he would cut off his own hand before he would hurt her.

But she did not appear to be hurting. In fact, he would interpret the expression on her face as distinctly pleasured. A terrible thought occurred to him. Had she been *saving* herself for marriage? And had she squandered her virginity on *this* marriage?

His conscience ached at the thought, but then his surging desire wiped away all but his need to see completion.

He couldn't last much longer. With one final plunge, he let himself go. She clutched him fiercely, holding him against her breasts as he spasmed, then slowly relaxed.

"Why didn't you tell me you were a virgin?"

Chapter Eleven

Rats. Amelia had hoped against hope that Nick, in the throes of passion, wouldn't notice and save her this awkward situation. "I didn't want you to know," she said as he moved to lie beside her. "And, no, I wasn't saving myself for any particular reason. It's just been awfully difficult to have intimate relationships in my situation. My sisters managed, but somehow I didn't."

He slid an arm beneath her and held her in a protective embrace that warmed her, physically and emotionally. "I would have been gentler if I'd—"

"Oh, no, Nick, you were perfect. Everything was fine."

"I hurt you."

"It was not a big deal. Besides, it was soon forgotten when everything started feeling...better." She traced a design with her finger on his chest, testing the texture of the diamond-shaped pattern of coarse hair there. "Is this where you were shot?" She lightly rubbed a strip of scar tissue along his ribs.

Nick tensed. "How did you know about that?"

"Grandfather told me. He said you were a war hero."

Nick moved her hand away from the scar. ''More like a guy in the wrong place at the wrong time.''

''Was it serious?''

''I'm still here, aren't I?'' He relaxed again, but apparently she'd discovered another topic of conversation that was taboo.

There were so many things about him she would like to explore. A lifetime wouldn't provide enough hours to do it.

Certainly six months wouldn't be enough.

She'd known this would happen. She'd known that if she slept with Nick, she would start wishing for things that could never be. But she was still glad they'd made love. Nick was a man starving for intimacy. He'd cut himself off from his emotional self after the tragedy of losing his family.

Still, sex wasn't the same as opening up emotionally. Nick had been a fabulous and considerate lover, bringing her more pleasure than she'd ever dared hope for. But she sensed that he held something back from her. He gave freely of his body, but not of his soul. Then again, touching could lead to trusting, and trusting could lead to more emotional intimacy.

Shoot, why should he trust her? She'd misled him so terribly in Palemeir. If she had it to do over again, she would level with him from the beginning.

Which led her to her current lack of honesty. Had she learned anything from her mistakes?

''Nick, there's something I simply must tell you before this goes any further.'' She plowed ahead, giving him no opportunity to stall her. ''King Easton has decided to name me heir to the throne of Korosol. Someday, not too soon, I hope, I'll be queen.''

Her announcement was greeted by absolute silence.

Amelia propped herself up on her shoulder so she could see Nick's face. His eyes were closed, his face relaxed, his breathing slow and regular.

He was fast asleep.

She'd heard about this, but she'd never thought it was so literally true, that a guy would fall unconscious thirty seconds after he found satisfaction. She could have been miffed, but given what poor Nick had been through this night, his exhaustion was perfectly understandable.

But she'd gone and wasted a perfectly good confession. Now she'd have to wait until morning to work up the courage and repeat herself. But she would do it, no more excuses.

AS THE LAST VESTIGES of his dreamworld melted away, Nick became aware of the warm, soft body pressed against his.

Oh, heaven help him. He'd made love to the princess, the virgin princess. Sure, it's what he'd wanted to do from the first time he'd laid eyes on her. But now that the deed was done, he had second thoughts about the wisdom of it.

The physical act of making love had had a far more profound effect on him than he wanted to admit. It certainly wasn't the first time he'd slept with a woman since Monette's death, but it was the first time he'd *felt* something. Of course, he'd been all worked up over the near tragedy with Josie, making it far easier for Amelia to get under his skin.

It would be so easy to open up to Amelia, to pour out his hurt and rage and guilt and fear and let her heal him. But he wasn't altogether sure he *could* be healed. Some things scarred a man forever, and opening up the old wound would accomplish nothing more than renewing the pain.

That he could do without.

Amelia was still sleeping soundly, and with an angelic smile on her face. His chest ached just watching her.

This was getting dicey. He had to get away from her and collect the pieces of his heart that were still left.

He slid out of bed, put on his shorts and went to check on the kids. Jakob, more subdued than usual, sat on the bed playing with some toy cars, running them up the mountains and valleys produced by his sleeping sister under the covers. Josie slept, oblivious, which gave Nick a moment of anxiety until he saw she was breathing easily.

Jakob stopped playing and observed Nick silently, his usual exuberance absent. Nick had never quite known what to make of Jakob's unabashed adoration of him, which Nick had done nothing to earn. But at this moment he missed it.

"How are you this morning, buddy?" Nick asked, trying to sound cheerful. "Looks like the storm is over and the sun is out."

Jakob merely gave the porthole a suspicious look.

Nick could only imagine how scared he must have been last night when the porthole gave way, sending a torrent of water into the Blue Cabin with the force of Niagara Falls.

"Are you going to yell at Josie?" Jakob finally asked.

"What? Oh. No, no, I'm not. I thought Auntie Mellie explained that to you. I was upset, and I got angry when I shouldn't have. I'm sorry if it frightened you."

"I wasn't scared."

"That's because you're a very brave boy."

Josie stirred and rolled over to observe Nick warily.

"How are you feeling, Josie?"

Immediately her eyes teared up. Oh, great. Nick could handle anything but tears from women or children. Josie hardly ever cried. She must really be worked up.

"You don't have to cry," he said. "I'm not mad anymore, although I hope you do understand now why we have strict rules on the boat. It can be very dangerous on the ocean."

Josie nodded. "I lost my Keds in the ocean."

"Is that what you're worried about? We'll get you some more, next port we pull into. What do you want for breakfast?"

"Cornflakes?" Josie asked hopefully.

Thank goodness Jules had bought some at the last port. "I think we can manage. Jakob?"

"Bananas."

"Absolutely."

As for himself, he could devour a dozen eggs and a side of bacon. He was quickly coming to understand and appreciate the American fascination with fat- and cholesterol-laden breakfasts, and he'd certainly worked up an appetite over the past twelve hours.

He'd been hoping to catch Amelia still in bed when he returned to their cabin, but she was already up, the shower running. He hadn't meant for her to wake up alone.

She emerged a few minutes later, fully clothed, wet

hair wrapped in a towel. Their gazes met, and her expression could only be described as cautious.

So she did have some reservations.

He skirted the corner of the bed, walked straight to her and kissed her soundly. "If I hadn't just promised the kids breakfast, I'd tumble you right back into that bed and have my wicked way with you."

"Oh, really? You think just because you deflowered me, that gives you the right to 'tumble' me, as you put it, anytime you like?"

"Uh…" He didn't have a ready answer for that. Apparently she had more than mere reservations.

Then she smiled. "C'mon, Nick, I'm teasing. You can tumble me anytime, anywhere. But before you do, there are some things we need to talk about."

"What?"

She patted his rear. His muscles jumped, unaccustomed to the familiarity. "Take your shower. I'll get started feeding those ravenous children, and we can talk at breakfast."

Nick wondered, all through his shower and shave, all through putting on clothes, what Amelia wanted to talk about. Men were supposed to break out in hives when a woman said that to them. He wasn't exactly that bad off, because she hadn't made it sound that serious, but he did wonder.

When he made it to the galley, Amelia already had breakfast well under way. The kids were working on bowls of cereal, Jakob's amply covered with bananas, and Amelia had large quantities of eggs and bacon on the griddle and biscuits in the oven, making him wonder if she was a mind reader.

"The guys already ate," she announced. "So it's just us."

"How's the captain? And Jules?"

"Everyone looks shipshape this morning, except Dave, who didn't get much sleep last night, poor guy."

Nick poured orange juice for everyone, coffee for himself, then helped Amelia with the bacon and eggs. Like a well-oiled machine, they had breakfast on the table in seconds flat, never spilling or colliding in the small galley.

At the table, Nick reminded them they should say grace, and even though he wasn't big on praying, he thanked God for not letting any of them drown last night. For that he earned a small smile from Josie.

"There's something I need to discuss with you," Amelia announced after they'd had a few bites of egg.

"Uh-oh," Josie said. "Does this mean we have to leave the table?"

"No," Amelia said, "because this is something that affects you, too."

Nick's senses were on red alert. Amelia sounded outwardly cheerful, but by now he knew her well enough, he could see she was a seething bundle of nerves beneath the surface.

"I'm sure you've all been wondering what King Easton is doing in America," she began.

"I haven't," Jakob said.

"Shh. Don't interrupt," Nick said.

"Well, the fact is that, since his son Byrum died last year, he's been a little nervous about who will succeed him on the throne."

"You mean who'll be king after him?" Josie asked.

"Yes, king...or queen."

"I don't blame him for being nervous," Nick said.

''That Markus is a wolf in sheep's clothing, if you ask me.''

''Who's a wolf?'' Jakob asked.

''Never mind,'' Nick said. ''Amelia, continue, please.''

''That's just it,'' she said, pausing to take a bite of bacon. ''For whatever reason, Easton doesn't believe Markus would make a good king. So he's decided to choose someone else.''

''Uh-huh.'' Nick laid down his fork as a sense of foreboding descended on him. This couldn't possibly be leading where he thought it was.

''What's a successor?'' Jakob asked.

''It means the next in line,'' Amelia said, picking up a napkin and wiping some jelly from Jakob's mouth in a gesture that had become unbelievably automatic for a woman who had only days ago acquired children. ''And it's me.''

''You're going to be queen?'' Josie's eyes just about popped out of her head.

Amelia looked down at her plate. ''It appears so. Nothing's official yet, but the king has made his choice known to the family.''

Josie sprang from her chair, upsetting her milk, but given the shocking news, no one made a move to clean it up. ''I knew it!'' she squealed. ''If you're a queen, that makes me a princess because you're my moth—because I'm your daughter!''

Nick wanted to refute Josie's claim to royal status before it got out of control, but somehow no words were making it past his throat. He was still in shock.

He was married to the future queen of Korosol.

A high buzzing started inside his head. Amelia was saying something else, explaining the circumstances more fully, while Josie was going off like a sparkler and asking whether she got to live at the palace and wear a crown and have her picture in the newspapers and wishing she had a ballerina tutu because she thought that was what princesses should wear.

Nick wasn't absorbing any of it. He couldn't quite get past the fact that his darling bride, with whom he had so recently consummated their marriage, had deceived him. Again.

Oh, she hadn't out-and-out lied to him. She hadn't told him she *wouldn't* be queen. But in his book, lies of omission were still lies.

His temper bubbled just below the surface, but he refused to explode in front of the children. They'd seen enough of that last night. He set his napkin on the table and scooted out from the banquette where he sat.

"Nick?" Amelia asked worriedly.

"I'm going up for air. Alone," he added when she started to get up, too.

On deck, the sun shone with mocking cheerfulness, sparkling on a smooth, blue sea as if last night's storms had never happened. Captain Lammas was at the helm, looking a bit sheepish. He offered Nick a two-fingered wave, then looked away, as if sensing Nick was in no mood for company. Nick supposed he should apologize for poisoning the man with saffron, but he would do it later.

He walked to the bow, where the wind and a slight salt spray hit him in the face, hoping the elements might wash away his horror.

He's married a queen, or an almost-queen, and the implications were staggering. The low-key divorce they'd talked about was an impossibility now. Once the news was made public that Amelia was heir to the throne of Korosol, all hell would break loose. Their lives would not be their own. And when the six months was over and it was time for them to part company, he would forever go down in history as the man who divorced Queen Amelia.

Then there was Josie to think about. As the queen's adopted daughter she might not be an official princess, but she would have some status in the royal family. Certainly, both children would be welcome at the palace. But if he divorced Amelia, the children's status would be zilch. Josie might never forgive him.

Why the hell had Amelia chosen to deliver this news in front of the kids, anyway? Damn, he knew the answer to that. If she'd told him in private, he might have lost his temper, and she knew it. The children had proved a good buffer.

He breathed in deeply of the salt air, but it didn't cool him down. It might take several icy showers to diminish his temper this time.

"I THINK YOU MADE Uncle Nick mad," Josie said, playing with her now-soggy cereal.

"Yes, I'm afraid I did," Amelia agreed as she started clearing the table. Jakob had gone into the saloon with his beloved cars, so it was just the two girls.

"Just because you're going to be a queen? I think that's neat."

"He wasn't expecting it. I guess I should have told him before the wedding."

"Will we get to live at the palace? Could I have a pony, maybe?"

Amelia's heart squeezed painfully. "Oh, Josie,

honey, this is so hard to explain. I'm not sure you'll understand it.''

"Understand what?"

Amelia sat down, abandoning the dish clearing. "You know that most people get married because they fall in love and want to spend the rest of their lives together, right?"

Josie nodded.

"It was a little different for Uncle Nick and me. We got married the first time, in Palemeir, so we could legally adopt you and take you and Jakob to a safer place."

"I know. I remember. Then you left us."

"I had to. No, that's not really true. I chose to leave because I thought it was the best thing at the time."

"Why?"

"For a lot of reasons that aren't important now."

"But you married Uncle Nick again. Don't you love him?"

Now *there* was a loaded question. She had great admiration and respect for Nick. She was fond of him. And if she was honest with herself, she'd fallen a little bit in love with him the first day she met him. But she hadn't let herself fall all the way. It was some form of self-preservation instinct. Maybe she sensed that he could not return her love, not in the way she needed to be loved by a man, and that was why she held back.

But how could she explain that to a seven-year-old?

"I think the world of Uncle Nick. He's a very, very good man, a real hero. But we aren't in love. We got married the second time so he could keep you and Jakob."

Josie took some time to absorb this. She didn't look too happy about it. "But you could fall in love, couldn't you?"

"It would be very nice if we could. Unfortunately, real life isn't like the fairy tales you read. Some things just aren't meant to be, and happily-ever-after just isn't in the cards for me and Nick. The fact is, we were planning to get a divorce after six months, or as soon as the Ministry of Family says it's okay for Nick to keep you."

Josie's eyes teared up. "Then I won't get to be a princess?"

"You'll always be my princess."

"That's not the same," Josie said sharply. "I was my papa's princess, too, but that didn't make me a real princess."

"When I live at the palace, you and Jakob can come visit me anytime you want. I'll make sure there's a room always ready, just for you."

"It's not the same!" Josie shouted. "I'm really, really, really mad at you!" She bolted from the table, darting into the saloon. Amelia followed in time to see her leaping over Jakob and his trucks and heading for her cabin.

"Josie, wait!" Amelia chased after her, but realized it was too late when she heard the cabin door slam. If Josie was like this at age seven, what would she be like when she hit puberty? That was a sobering thought.

"Hey, you broke my truck!"

"What? Oh." Belatedly, Amelia realized that in her haste she'd stepped on one of Jakob's toys. Flattened it, in fact.

"Oh, I'm so sorry, Jakob. Let's move your racetrack over in that corner, away from the place people walk.''

"It was my favorite!" he wailed.

Oh, dear. She hadn't realized this was such a serious tragedy. Jakob was normally so good-natured, nothing fazed him. "I'm very, very sorry. I'll buy you a new one, okay?"

"It won't be the same."

What was it with kids wanting things to be "the same"?

"Then I'll buy you any kind of toy car or truck you want, okay?" Amelia said a little desperately. She wasn't in the habit of bribing children, but it seemed a bad time to alienate little Jakob along with everyone else. She tried to hug him and comfort him, but he was having none of it. He pulled out of her embrace and ran crying toward his cabin.

Great. *Everybody* was mad at her.

After finishing the breakfast cleanup, Amelia decided she'd let Nick sulk long enough. They needed to talk, whether he wanted to or not.

Abovedecks, the breeze was soft and warm. They'd definitely passed into a different climate zone. She could see land in the distance, and wondered idly exactly where they were. She didn't have a clue.

The weather was beautiful, though, and a seagull flew alongside the yacht, matching its pace, gliding so close Amelia could almost reach out and touch it. Then it banked away, probably looking elsewhere for handouts.

She walked along the deck until she found her quarry. Nick was at the very front of the boat, elbows on the railing, staring out to sea. She watched him for a few minutes while he was unaware of her presence, unable to help but appreciate what a gorgeous specimen of man he was, and what a dolt she was to have mismanaged her relationship with him so badly.

Last night she'd found a little slice of heaven in his arms. He'd been tender, attentive, not to mention skillful, making it easy for her to fantasize they were a real married couple. But having him angry at her, perhaps despising her, was more like a fairly large slice of hell.

She didn't move or speak or make any noise, but somehow he knew she was there. He turned and slowly allowed his gaze to meet hers. The only greeting he gave her was a slight lifting of one eyebrow, almost as if he was challenging her to approach him.

Well, let him do his worst to her, she thought as she approached him. Whatever he dished out, she probably deserved it.

"Are you ready to talk to me?" she asked. "Or would you like to brood some more?"

"You should be glad I'm brooding. The alternative isn't very pleasant."

"Go ahead and yell, if it'll make you feel better. The wind will carry away your words, so no one will hear. No one but me, that is."

He stared at her a moment. Then suddenly he exploded. "What were you thinking, keeping this a secret from me?"

She took a step back, surprised even though she'd told him to yell. She hadn't really expected him to do it.

"How long have you known you were the future queen?" he demanded when she didn't answer his first question right away.

"If you'll give me half a chance, I'll try to explain."

"I'd like to hear your explanation."

"I've known since before you arrived in New York. I didn't tell you right away because the information is highly confidential. For obvious reasons, the king doesn't want all of Korosol to know he's choosing someone other than Markus as his heir, at least not until he makes an official announcement along with an official reason."

Nick crossed his arms, as if to indicate that so far this was the lamest explanation he'd ever heard.

"I didn't tell you before the wedding because, frankly, I didn't believe I would need to. Grandfather wasn't thrilled about the first, illegal marriage, and he was positively livid when I told him I was marrying you again. I was sure he no longer wanted me as his heir."

"Which was exactly the result you wanted."

"Let's just say my feelings about becoming queen are ambivalent. But I didn't purposely set out to disappoint Grandfather."

"Apparently you didn't."

"He seems to hold you in very high regard."

Nick turned away from her and stared out to sea again.

"I'd marry you all over again, even if the king had disowned me. And you don't regret the decision, either. You'd do whatever it took to keep Josie and Jakob."

"I had other choices."

"Oh, right. Running off to Canada, living in the woods on nuts and berries."

"I could have done a little better than that. Anyway, I might prefer freezing my buns off in a Canadian forest, eating pinecones, to being a *royal prince consort.* How could you do that to me? How could you put me in that position?''

''I honestly believed you wouldn't be in that position. Given Grandfather's reaction to the wedding announcement, I thought it was a cinch he'd snatch that throne away from me so fast my head would spin. I was completely shocked by his sudden reversal—I mean, in the span of a few days you went from villainous mercenary to national hero in his eyes. It just didn't occur to me he would still allow me to be his heir, much less want it with so much enthusiasm.''

''So you're telling me you treated this whole thing like a lottery. Or...or Russian roulette.''

''Oh, so now being married to me is like a bullet to the brain? Thank you, thanks very much. Listen, buddy, there are millions of men who might actually like being married to a queen. Just what is so bad about it?''

''It's not me I'm worried about. It's the children. I promised their mother I would give them a normal, wholesome life. As members of the royal family, even adopted, they'll be subjected to constant scrutiny, constant publicity. For the rest of their lives, they won't be able to make a move without someone watching and commenting.''

''That's ridiculous. You told me the people in your village don't care about royalty. 'A flurry of curiosity seekers at first, but it'll be old news in a few days.' I believe those were your exact words.''

''The children may not live in Montavi their whole lives. What about when they grow up?''

''When they grow up? Nick, when they grow up,

no one will even remember we were married. We're divorcing in six months. Five months and three weeks. Or have you forgotten?''

"I haven't forgotten. But here's news for you, my lovely wife. I will not go through the rest of my life and into posterity as the jerk who dumped and divorced the queen of Korosol. I will not explain to my children, particularly Josie, that it's my fault we didn't get to live in the palace and wear ballet tutus all day long.

"If there's any divorcing to be done, you'll have to do it.''

Chapter Twelve

Nick was initially pleased with his own mandate. Amelia needed to learn that her deceptions—though well motivated in her mind—had consequences. If she wanted to play fast and easy with his future, his children's future, let it affect her own future as well.

He wouldn't fight the divorce, but he would make damn sure she was the one who did the deed. Let her play the villain to the press. He could play the part of the jilted husband. He certainly had no intention of marrying again any time soon, so his legal bonds to Amelia would pose no problems. He could wait her out, if she was squeamish about starting divorce proceedings.

Eventually she would have to do something about him. As queen she would be expected to have children of her own, and he had no plans to procreate further. He had his hands full with Josie and Jakob.

The thought of Amelia marrying and having children with someone else, some duke or maybe a prince from another country, just made him angrier, though it shouldn't have.

"What makes you think I'm in such a hurry to divorce?" she asked.

"Well, aren't you? You bring it up often enough."

"You're the one who almost had a stroke when you heard we had to stay together for six months. I have no problem with that. In fact, we can stay married indefinitely for all I care. After you get custody of Josie and Jakob, we can live apart, as married royal couples have done for centuries. No one will think a thing of it."

"Ah, but you're forgetting one thing, my indifferent one. If we stay married, what happens when you're expected to produce an heir?"

That stopped her—for about five seconds. But her dander was up, and she wasn't about to concede this argument. "Would it be such a struggle for us to produce a child? Obviously we have the mechanical aspects down."

Mechanical aspects. Interesting euphemism for the incredible passion they'd shared only a few hours ago. It would be easy for Nick to let memories of their sensual encounter soften him, so he put it right out of his mind.

"Get this straight, Princess. No child of mine is going to be the ruler of Korosol. The very thought is abhorrent to me."

"Why?"

"It's not a fate I would wish on my worst enemy, much less my flesh and blood. The kid's life wouldn't be his own. You've said yourself what a hardship it was, being raised in the public eye. Now imagine that ten times over, and imagine that boy or girl's childhood. Besides, royal families are all screwed up."

"I beg your pardon."

"Not yours, in particular. You and your family are all right, despite the odds."

"Oh, thanks."

"But look at your cousin Markus. A complete wastrel. Your father died prematurely—"

"That had nothing to do with his—"

"—your uncle Prince Byrum and his wife got blown up in a jeep accident—"

"That was a simple—"

"—and your other uncle Prince James is a thrice-married alcoholic."

"That is a gross oversimplification. Anyway, every family has a few bad apples, a few tragedies."

"I'm not having children with you, so just get it out of your head. You'll have to find another prince consort."

"Fine! If you don't want to consort, we won't consort!" She turned and stalked away, and by some illogical twist of fate, she took a tiny sliver of Nick's heart with her.

He hadn't meant for things to get so out of hand. He hadn't meant to insult her whole family or indicate that he found having children with her a repugnant idea. Amelia, the woman, wasn't the problem. He just didn't want more children, period. He scarcely had the inner strength to handle the ones that had fallen into his lap, and he certainly would have nothing left to give yet another, particularly under the stressful conditions a royal birth would bring.

He definitely hadn't meant to turn her off the idea of *consorting*. Just because they weren't destined to remain married through eternity, was that any reason for them not to enjoy the time they were together?

With a sigh, he realized there *was* a reason, and Amelia had summed it up nicely a few days ago when she'd pointed out that they might be legally married but they weren't committed. He could make love to a woman without commitment, as most men could, but he understood that women's brains worked differently.

He saw the months ahead stretching before them, dry and sterile, and knew there was nothing he could do to change that. It was not in Amelia's nature to share her most intimate secrets with him when they were not committed for life.

Last night had been a fluke, a natural physical release demanded by the high emotions of a life-and-death crisis. Even if he hadn't just alienated Amelia for life, he probably couldn't have expected her to start jumping in to bed with him at every opportunity.

He might have been able to live with that, barely, but he couldn't live with her hating him for the next six months. He was going to have to implement some damage control.

Of course, he hadn't the slightest idea how to do that.

AMELIA, sniffing back angry tears, headed straight for the bridge, where she found Captain Lammas on watch, relaxed but alert, sipping coffee.

"Ah, good morning, Your Highness. We should reach Bermuda by nightfall."

"Turn around."

"Pardon me?"

"Head back to New York, please. I'd like to return home as soon as possible."

"I understand your reluctance to sail in light of last night's storm, but—"

"No, it has nothing to do with the storm. I've just realized—" She stopped before she could give the

captain any real indication of matrimonial dishar-
mony. She could not afford to be selfish or petty here.
If word got out that her and Nick's marriage was anything but blissful, it might hurt his chances at keeping
the children. Whatever else happened, she couldn't
lose sight of her primary goal—keeping Josie and Jakob with Nick.

"Yes, Your Highness?"

"I've just realized I don't want to be away from
home for so long. Nick and I have many plans and
decisions to make, and I think we've relaxed
enough."

"It will be at least five days back to New York."

She was tempted to jump ship at the nearest port
and fly home. Five days cooped up with Nick when
she was so furious with him would be torture. But
she couldn't afford to arouse suspicion.

"Five days will be fine," she said, trying to sound
calm and serene. "Just don't dillydally."

"Yes, ma'am. Your Highness, I mean."

Amelia didn't even bother going into her standard
lecture about how he didn't have to call her that. It
was too exhausting, fighting who she was, and especially fighting the notion of who she was shortly to
become.

She was a future queen. How would Queen Amelia
deal with this situation?

She'd made a mistake, but she had already apolo-
gized, and she wasn't going to grovel. She would live
out this next six months with dignity, as a queen
should. She would lavish attention on the children,
but she would be honest with them about their future,
or lack thereof, with her.

When the six months was over and the children's

futures were secured, she would initiate divorce proceedings, because that was what Nick wanted. She would accept blame for the failure of the marriage and let him off the hook, then deal with the fallout as best she could. Meanwhile, she would request of the king that he delay announcing his choice of heir. He might change his mind once she sullied her reputation yet again by dumping her hero husband.

Because she could think of nothing else to do, Amelia went into the kitchen and got out the ingredients for chocolate chip cookies. She'd had no idea cooking and baking could be so much fun, and now she took solace in the comforting activities. Nick had given her that, and it was something of him she would have forever. He'd also initiated her into the world of lovemaking in the best way possible, and she could find it in her heart to be grateful for that, too, even if she was still mad at him.

Jules hung out with her for a little while. Though he'd been in the Carradignes' employ for a couple of years, now, she'd never really talked to him until this trip. But now that she was getting to know him, she realized he was truly committed to his role of protecting her, and he took it very seriously. He also had a wife and kids of his own, but he hadn't once complained about being separated from them for all this time.

"Do you miss your kids?" she asked after she'd slid two cookie sheets into the oven.

"Of course," he answered in between licking a beater. "But I call home on my cell phone every time we're in port." He laughed. "My daughter, Anya, said she drew a picture of me on the boat with the princess. I can't wait to see it."

Amelia's heart ached. She hadn't realized how badly she'd wanted a family of her own until she'd gotten a taste of it. Even the children's tantrums hadn't dampened her enthusiasm for family life. She'd take it all, the good and the bad.

She had one glimmer of hope. Nick said he wouldn't initiate divorce proceedings, that the dirty job belonged to her. Well, what if she didn't do it, either? They could stay married indefinitely, or at least longer than six months. Maybe…

It was hard to imagine. Not only was Nick furious with her, but he might never trust her again. How would her grandfather react when he discovered his heir's marriage was a minefield of misunderstandings and disagreements?

"Cookies?"

Amelia jumped, realizing she'd been lost in her own dismal thoughts for some time. Jules had slipped out of the kitchen with his usual quiet unobtrusiveness, and Jakob had slipped in. His face was a bit flushed from his recent crying bout, but other than that he looked perfectly normal, his usual cheerful, mischievous self.

"Chocolate chip," Amelia confirmed. "And I think there's one spoon left to lick."

Jakob's eyes lit up as Amelia handed him the dough-laden mixing spoon. She picked him up, carried him to the dining room and sat down with him. Nothing felt better than the warm, squirming body of a child in her lap.

For about the tenth time that morning, Amelia found herself near tears. She had known this would happen going into the marriage. She'd known she would bond more closely with the children, and that giving them up would be the most painful thing she'd ever done. But she hadn't known how painful.

A few minutes later, Amelia caught sight of Josie creeping into the saloon. She didn't approach Amelia and Jakob, just flopped down on the sofa, making sure everyone saw her sulking. The kitchen timer sounded. Amelia set Jakob down and went to pull the chocolate-studded cookies from the oven.

"Cookies!" Jakob shouted excitedly, jumping from one foot to another.

"We have to let them cool first," Amelia said as she loosened the cookies with a spatula. "Five minutes."

"Can we have ice cream, too?"

Amelia looked at her watch. It was just after ten in the morning. They shouldn't be eating cookies, much less ice cream. Oh, what the hell. Nick was awfully strict with them, and they *were* on vacation. Would it hurt if she spoiled them just this once?

"Maybe one spoonful of ice cream. Go ask your sister if she wants some, too."

By the time Nick reappeared, both kids were sitting at the dining table eating cookie-ice-cream sandwiches. He did an almost comical double take, then turned to Amelia, grabbed her arm and dragged her into the kitchen. "What the hell are you feeding my children?"

Amelia shook her dish towel at him. "Do not use that tone with me, Nicholas Standish. They're my children, too, at least while we're married. Or have you forgotten that we both adopted them?"

Apparently he had, because he lost all his steam. He turned away from her, as if collecting himself, then turned back. "I've tried to limit their sweets to a reasonable level."

"Two cookies and a dab of ice cream isn't unreasonable. Yes, it's a bit of an indulgence, but give them a break. They're on vacation."

He gave the cookie treats one last censorious look before changing the subject. "The boat turned around."

"I asked Captain Lammas to head back for New York. I've had about enough of this honeymoon stuff, haven't you?"

Nick nodded tersely, then stalked to the back of the boat, presumably to their cabin.

FOR THE NEXT FIVE DAYS, the boat was like an armed camp. Nick took to staying up late, reading in the saloon. He came to their cabin usually after Amelia had fallen asleep, quietly making his pallet on the floor.

Once or twice, Amelia considered seducing him. Hitting him while he was asleep and vulnerable, getting him all worked up before he was really alert, then hoping that, in typical male fashion, he would carry through. Her body, once awakened, craved Nick's touch, yearned for the completion only he had given her. But she always talked herself out of it. If he rejected her, she would be devastated.

Amelia and the children usually ate together, but Nick, more often than not, took his dinner with the crew. He stopped cooking altogether, leaving that task to Amelia.

"Teaching me to cook was an evil plot on your uncle Nick's part," Amelia said to Josie as the girl helped with dinner one night. "Once I had the basics down, he could stick me with all the work."

Josie rolled her eyes. "Typical male."

Amelia laughed. Where on earth had Josie picked that up? From TV, probably. Apparently Montavi didn't have a TV station, and no cable, either. She'd been fascinated with television ever since arriving in America.

The girl had come around slightly, no longer scowling and pouting twenty-four hours a day. But Amelia knew it would be a long time before she won Josie's trust again, if ever.

As the *Duchess* moved farther north, the weather got cool and misty. Everyone broke out their long pants and sweaters and jackets, and their moods descended with the temperatures. By the time they arrived at the marina, smiles were a thing of the past.

Unfortunately, news of their impending return had somehow reached the press, and a group of photographers and reporters were on the dock to greet them late one Monday night as they disembarked.

Nick cast a warning look at Amelia, and by silent agreement they put on a show, smiling hollow smiles, their arms loosely around each other.

"I'd like to stay and talk," Amelia said graciously to the assembled reporters, "but we have a couple of cranky kids to put to bed."

The children were obligingly cranky, with Josie sullen and Jakob crying.

One reporter's voice emerged louder than the others. "Did you enjoy your honeymoon?"

Amelia was appalled to realize the voice was attached to none other than Krissy Katwell. The columnist had made it some sort of personal mission to dog the Carradignes and humiliate them. No matter what Amelia answered, she feared it would somehow come out bad in print.

Nick stepped in smoothly. "'Enjoy' isn't the term I would use. Much too pale a word." He flashed a distinctly lascivious smile, then whisked Amelia and the children to the waiting limousine while Jules kept the press at bay.

"That was a nice performance," Amelia said tartly when they were safely behind tinted glass.

"It wasn't a lie, was it?"

Amelia sighed. "No. It's a good thing we're both such fine actors. We'll have to put on quite a show once we're back at the penthouse."

"Why? Your family knows the situation."

"Not my mother—not really. She knows about your problems with the Ministry of Family, but I sort of told her we were marrying for love. Anyway," she rushed on, "there are servants to worry about. Don't forget Krissy Katwell's spy."

Nick checked to see that both children had nodded off. "Are you telling me we have to play the part of the devoted couple?"

"If you don't want any stories getting back to the Ministry of Family, yes."

This just got worse and worse. "Then let's go back to Montavi as soon as possible. At least we'll have some privacy at the house. You can have your own bedroom, and there aren't any servants to worry about."

"Grandfather wouldn't be very pleased about my changing residence just now. I'm sort of…under his tutelage at the moment. I'm a queen-in-training."

"Great. Just great."

"Anyway, I'll have to move to Korosol soon enough. After that, I'll hardly ever get to see my family. That's why I want to stay in New York, for just a little while longer."

"How long?"

"Until Grandfather says it's time to go. Please, Nick. We'll get Josie a tutor—school won't be a problem for her. And if you want, we can get our own apartment, so we won't be on display so much."

Nick's jaw worked. Amelia understood his desire to return to his village home. His whole world had been turned upside down during the past few weeks. The children were disoriented and crankier than they had been when they arrived, probably because their routine had been so disrupted.

But her world had been shaken up, too. Very little remained of the life she'd carved for herself before the king had picked her as heir to the throne. She really, really needed her mother, her sisters and Hester right now. They were the only constants left, and she wouldn't have them for long.

"We'll stay a while longer," Nick finally said.

"Thank you. I'll get to work on finding a first-rate tutor right away. And we'll get the children into a better routine, so they'll feel more secure."

Nick nodded, then looked out the window at the lights of Manhattan passing by, and Amelia wondered if he was thinking the same thing she was. How could the children ever feel secure when their "parents" were scarcely on speaking terms?

NICK DIDN'T KNOW how things had gotten so out of hand. He'd intended to apologize for losing his temper, and for saying some less-than-sensitive things about Amelia's family. He'd fully intended to call a truce, to work his way back into her good graces.

But somehow the apology never got made, and the walls between them just got taller and thicker. He didn't know how he was going to survive the next few months like this. Something had to give.

Though it was after midnight, Charlotte was up to greet them when they arrived home.

"Looks like you all got some sun," she said cheerfully as she ushered them inside the penthouse and instructed Quincy in which room to put the luggage. She wore a satin robe and matching slippers, but her hair was neatly styled. He'd never seen Lady Charlotte any way but perfectly poised. "I know it's late, and you're probably keen to go to bed, but I've made some herbal tea. Won't you stay up and tell me all about your trip?"

Nick exchanged a look with Amelia, who stepped in. "We really need to get the children to bed."

Hester appeared in the foyer at that moment, in flannel robe and hair curlers. "Now, now, I can take care of the little ones. You know I've been itching to get my hands on them. Come to Aunt Hester, now."

Jakob went from Nick's arms to Hester's without protest, and Josie, drowsy but awake on her own two feet, willingly gave her hand to Hester and allowed herself to be led upstairs. Poor child probably couldn't wait to escape the tension between her parents—and to sleep in a room that didn't rock.

Nick followed Amelia and her mother to the kitchen, feeling awkward and inadequate. If Charlotte expected him to be some ideal husband who would make Amelia happy the rest of her life, she had a big disappointment coming.

He decided to let Amelia handle the conversation. He would answer questions put directly to him, but otherwise he would just sip his tea and keep quiet.

"I'm quite furious that I only got the one postcard from you," Charlotte said.

"Well, Mother, we *were* on our honeymoon."

"Yes, quite. But we were all so anxious…"

To hear whether the bride and groom were cozying up or coming after each other with the galley knives, he suspected.

"We weren't in port very much," Amelia said. "We liked the boat so much, we just kept sailing."

"Did you have any problems?"

"One storm," Amelia said breezily. Nick hoped Charlotte wouldn't demand a full report from Captain Lammas, or she would find out all that Amelia had kept from her.

"What was the best thing about the trip?" Charlotte asked.

"Nick taught me to cook."

Charlotte gasped. "Really?"

"I learned how to cook a roast, and steam any kind of vegetable, and I can make pasta and pastry and cookies—my cakes aren't any great shakes, though. But breakfast—I can make anything for breakfast. Pancakes, omelettes…"

Charlotte shot an accusing look at Nick. "Ten days with you, and my daughter's turned into a galley slave." But then she patted his hand and smiled. "I've put you both in Amelia's suite. The decor is a bit feminine for you, Nick, but we can get the decorator in to change things."

"That won't be necessary," Nick said. "I'm sure I'll like it just fine the way it is."

"I gave each of the children his and her own room. Josie's getting to be a big girl, and I'm sure she wants her own space. I want them to feel that this place is their home, not some hotel."

"Thank you, Mother," Amelia said, giving Charlotte a kiss on the cheek. "You know, of course, that we can't stay here forever."

Charlotte teared up. "I know. Even if Easton weren't taking you away from me—oh, you've told Nick, haven't you?"

Nick forced his jaw to relax. "She told me."

"Well, even if you didn't have to go away because of that, I've reconciled myself to the fact that Korosol is Nick's home, and perhaps your destiny, darling. But I don't have to like it."

"I thought you were all for me being queen," Amelia said.

"I was, until I realized I won't get to see you."

"You'll come visit as often as you want."

"It won't be the same. But I guess every mother has to let her babies follow their own dreams."

Amelia hugged her mother, leaving Nick feeling like a fifth wheel. He understood better now why Amelia wanted to stay in New York a while longer, but that didn't mean he had to like it. How could he and Amelia possibly convince anyone for long that they were happily married? Krissy Katwell had spies, and she would no doubt be delighted to report that the newest royal marriage was on the rocks. Any such story would immediately be repeated by Korosol's tabloids, and he was quite confident the dragon ladies at the Ministry of Family read a steady diet of tabloids.

"You two look done in," Charlotte said. "Go to

bed, and you can tell me everything about the trip tomorrow. Well, maybe not everything.'' She tittered with laughter as she led the way out of the kitchen. Amelia blushed, whether from embarrassment or some other intense emotion, he didn't know.

Amelia silently led him up the stairs and down a hallway to her suite. Or rather, *their* suite. He had to restrain himself from laughing as he entered. Charlotte hadn't been kidding; the room was a riot of floral prints and pastels, every surface covered in silk or satin. Even the carpeting was pink.

''Don't say a word. We'll redecorate, as Mother suggested. It needs it anyway. I haven't changed the room since I was in high school.''

''Why not?'' he asked, suddenly curious. Most women, faced with an unlimited source of funds, would refurnish every six months.

''Truthfully? I'm not usually home enough to worry about it. I've spent a lot of years living out of a suitcase.'' She sank onto the bed, as if she didn't have the energy to go one step farther.

''Do you miss the travel?''

''Terribly.''

''Perhaps when you're queen, you can organize some goodwill missions. Use your high profile to draw attention to suffering children.''

She looked up at him, a glimmer of hope in her eyes. ''Yes, I could do that, couldn't I?''

''I know being a queen isn't your ideal future, but there has to be some advantages. What's the good of being a monarch if you can't throw your weight around to get help for people who need it?''

''Don't let Grandfather hear you say that.''

''I'm not afraid of him.''

"Well, I am. Intimidated, anyway. He doesn't abuse his power, but he could."

A sobering thought, but Nick was too tired to think about it right now. He had more immediate concerns—like sleeping arrangements. The carpet looked plenty soft, but... "What are you doing?" Amelia had gone to a closet and pulled out a sheet, blanket and extra pillow. She was spreading the sheet over a chaise longue.

"I can't make you sleep on the floor anymore."

"I'm not sleeping on *that* thing." The delicate piece of furniture would probably break if he put his full weight on it. Not to mention it was less than five feet long, and he was over six.

"It's not for you, it's for me. I'll be perfectly comfortable."

"Amelia, let's be practical. It's a big bed. We can share it."

"No, thank you."

"We'll build a wall of pillows between us."

She gave him a look he couldn't interpret, then pulled a pair of pajamas out of a drawer and headed wordlessly into the bathroom.

He'd thought for a minute there she was softening. They'd actually been conversing almost pleasantly. But, no, the walls were there, strong as ever.

With a growl he stripped down to nothing, then grabbed the sheet and pillow off the chaise longue and threw them on the floor. Moments later he was under the sheet, feigning sleep. Just let her try to move him.

Chapter Thirteen

Amelia woke up stiff and sore. The chaise longue wasn't nearly as comfortable as she'd thought it would be. She looked over at Nick, who was sprawled on the floor on his stomach, snoring softly. The sheet covering him had ridden down to his hips, revealing his tan, well-muscled torso.

Neither of them had slept in the bed.

Amelia couldn't help but smile at the irony. They were two very strong-willed people. No wonder their relationship was so rocky.

He moved in his sleep and the sheet shifted lower, revealing the paler skin of his hip. Amelia found herself wishing fervently that he would thrash again, maybe throw off the sheet completely. She might not have the benefits of conjugal rights at the moment, but that didn't mean she couldn't appreciate the masculine contours of her husband's body.

She sighed, remembering how that body had felt to her touch, first warm and soft, then slicked with sweat as their lovemaking had taken on heat and energy. She recalled the exact texture of his hair, soft and silky despite the military cut. She could almost feel again the rasp of his jaw against her face and neck...and other places.

A persistent ache grew inside her. What would happen if she tiptoed over to him and lay down beside him? Would he welcome her as a husband should his wife? Would he reject her? Or would he simply view her as a handy means of release?

It was this last possibility that stopped her from following through with her fantasy. She could handle rejection, but she couldn't handle making love to Nick when he was clearly repelled by her outside the bedroom. True intimacy was part of a strong marriage. But plain old sex couldn't fix an ailing one.

With a sigh she sat up, stretched her aching muscles and headed into the bathroom. If she was lucky, she could shower, dress and escape before Nick even woke up.

No such luck. He was gone when she came out of the bathroom. She dressed quickly, knowing he was probably checking on the kids. She hoped they wouldn't be disoriented with the change of venue.

She found all three of them in Josie's room, which surprised Amelia with its ruffly canopy bed perfectly suited to a little-girl princess. Furthermore, the room was lined with dolls and stuffed animals.

Charlotte, or someone, had completely redecorated for Josie's benefit. Amelia suspected Jakob's room had also been transformed.

The trio didn't see Amelia as she peeked into the room. Nick sat against the bed's headboard, one child on either side of him, and he read from a classic children's book. Josie and Jakob appeared to be enthralled.

The only thing missing was any sign of physical

affection. Nick should have an arm around Josie, and Jakob should be in his lap. Those two children craved affection from their uncle Nick. But no matter how unfailingly concerned he was about the kids, no matter how fiercely he protected them, no matter how involved he was in their lives and committed to securing their futures, he didn't seem capable of making that leap of love. Hugs and kisses and words of love weren't a part of his makeup.

Amelia withdrew without making her presence known. Let them bond, without her. The stronger they connected with each other, the less traumatic it would be for them when she left.

Sniffing back those annoying tears, she headed for the kitchen.

"Amelia!" CeCe dropped the bagel on which she was spreading cream cheese and rushed over to hug her sister. "I didn't expect to see you up so early. Mother said you were exhausted last night."

"Couldn't sleep." Amelia hugged CeCe back. "How's the baby doing?"

"Fine. I feel great, though I'm hungry all the time. I used to skip breakfast. Of course, I can't do that anymore, doctor's orders, but I've found I'm suddenly ravenous for all sorts of horrible things like pancakes and omelettes. In fact, I've emptied out my own refrigerator. That's why I'm here, raiding yours."

"Let me fix you something more substantial, then," Amelia said, checking the huge double refrigerator for eggs and cheese and such.

"You?" CeCe laughed.

"Just watch." In mere seconds, Amelia was whipping eggs and grating cheese like a professional chef, while CeCe watched in amazement.

"Where did you learn that?"

"On my honeymoon. Nick taught me. If we hadn't taken over the cooking, we'd have been forced to eat canned soup three meals a day."

"Uh-oh, that sounds ominous."

"It's not as bad as all that." Amelia poured her egg concoction into the greased omelette pan. "We had a good time, although Jules was seasick, the captain had an allergic reaction that almost killed him, and Josie fell overboard in a storm and Nick had to jump in and save her. Oh, and the boat almost sank."

CeCe gasped. "You're making this up."

"I'm afraid not. Well, the boat didn't almost sink, but one of the cabins flooded. Don't say anything to Mother. She'll feel bad, since the yacht was her idea."

"I won't, but…oh, Amelia, tell me at least that you and Nick grew closer through all the adversity."

"Not exactly. We're not even sleeping together."

CeCe gasped again. "How are you going to bond if you don't sleep together?"

Amelia sprinkled grated cheese onto the omelette, then folded it in half with a spatula. "It doesn't work that way for me. I have to bond first, then sex."

"Don't tell me you haven't… Oh, never mind, I guess that's none of my business."

"CeCe, I wouldn't be unloading on you if I didn't want to talk about it. Yes, we have, and it was great. But that was before I told him I'm going to be queen. He is really, really displeased, and I guess I don't blame him."

"What's so wrong with that?"

"He objects for the same reasons you did when you were in the royal hot seat—he doesn't want himself or the children to be in the public eye, every move scrutinized, nothing private. It's a legitimate objection. I just wish I knew what to do about it.''

''There's no chance Grandfather will change his mind. He hasn't stopped talking about Nick since your wedding. He's already naming your children.''

Amelia flipped the omelette onto a plate, set it on the kitchen table in front of CeCe, then slumped into a chair. ''There won't be any children.''

''You aren't actually planning divorce, are you?'' CeCe asked in a whisper. ''Not now.''

''Truthfully, I don't know. Once he has custody of the children, we'll simply live separately, at least until I figure out what to do.''

CeCe reacted with such vehement horror, Amelia was almost afraid. ''You can't do that. That's no way to live. Do you want to be miserable your whole life?''

''A divorce would cause a huge scandal. Nick doesn't want to go down in the history books as the man who dumped a queen, and I don't blame him. And it would be difficult for me to initiate a divorce. Grandfather would never forgive me, and the citizens of Korosol would probably rise up and have me beheaded for jilting a hero like Nick.''

''This is positively medieval. Just tell Grandfather you don't want to be queen. That would solve everything.''

''I'm tempted, believe me. And maybe, if Nick loved me, I might give up the throne for him and the children. But I'm not giving it up just so I can have great sex.''

''You were always the dutiful one,'' CeCe commented as she took a bite of the omelette. "Oh my Lord, you *can* cook."

"It's not just duty. Nick pointed out to me that, as queen, I can help a lot more people than I could as plain old Melanie Lacey. Besides, if I turn my back on Korosol now, who would the king turn to?"

"Lucia, of course."

"Lucia would enjoy it for about five minutes."

"Lucia can take care of herself. Amelia, for once think of yourself. Do what's right for Amelia, not the king or your sister or all the starving children in the world."

Amelia took a bite of the cream-cheese bagel CeCe had abandoned in favor of the omelette. She'd thought of herself far too often these days. Her selfish decision to avoid confrontation and deceive Nick about her new status as future queen had gotten her into this mess. She didn't deserve to take the easy way out. Or, as Hester was fond of saying, she'd made her bed, now she could lie in it.

On the chaise longue.

"Listen, I've got to get to work," CeCe said, delicately wiping the corners of her mouth with a cloth napkin. "Shane and Mother are already there. They insist I sleep late because of the baby, but I feel very guilty about it."

Amelia smiled. "And you accuse *me* of being dutiful."

"Why don't the four of us have dinner tonight? Me, Shane, you and Nick."

"Oh, I don't think—"

"I insist. I want to get to know my new brother-in-law before you both run off to Korosol."

"All right," Amelia agreed uneasily, thinking that

a public appearance by the two of them every so often would help in creating an aura of marital bliss.

"We'll go to that new place in the Village everyone's raving about. I'll arrange everything."

That's just what worried Amelia.

NICK HAD HOPED he could sneak out of the penthouse without encountering anyone. He had plans to take the children to the Metropolitan Museum of Art to soak up a little culture. They'd watched far too many cartoon videos on the yacht, though he hadn't complained too much at the time because they were in danger of going stir-crazy.

He'd informed Amelia of their plans without inviting her, figuring she would be too busy with future-queen activities. She had suggested they take a security person with them, just in case. Their picture had appeared in the paper, after all. But he'd declined. He could take care of himself and the children just fine.

Unfortunately, they met up with King Easton in the foyer, just as he was heading for the embassy.

"Nicholas, my boy, I hadn't realized you were back," the king said, shaking Nick's hand heartily. "Did you enjoy the boat ride?"

"I almost drowned," Josie said.

Easton didn't seem to take that too seriously. "Indeed. Sounds most unfortunate. When will we be able to meet?"

"Meet?" Nick repeated, feeling a bit slow.

"We'll need to go over some things—rules of protocol for your new position, perhaps a meeting with an image consultant, and the public relations people, of course."

It was on the tip of Nick's tongue to shout, "Are you insane?" Just in time, he recalled to whom he was speaking. It was difficult to remember Easton was his king when the man was spouting such ridiculous stuff. An image consultant? He looked down at his wrinkled khaki slacks and battered athletic shoes. His image was just fine, thank you very much.

Instead, Nick said, "Let me know when it's convenient. I'll be there." No sense in antagonizing the king now. He would do enough of that when they actually got down to brass tacks—when he told the king what he could do with his prince-consort-grooming ambitions. Korosol, including its royal family, would have to take him as he was.

"And where is your bride this morning?" King Easton asked jovially. "Why isn't she accompanying you?"

"She has her own agenda for the day," Nick answered as diplomatically as possible.

"We ditched her," Jakob added helpfully.

Nick wanted to slap his hand over Jakob's mouth. Where had he heard such an expression?

"I don't have anything planned for her," Easton said, seemingly bothered by the fact that Nick and Amelia weren't together.

"Actually, I thought she could use some 'alone time' with her sisters and mother," Nick improvised. "The way we've come crashing into her life—well, it's an adjustment for all of us."

That was apparently the wrong thing to say. "You aren't getting along?"

"We're getting along very well," Nick lied. Josie looked at him reproachfully, and Nick knew he would have to explain this to her later.

The royal limousine was waiting at the curb. Easton asked politely if he could drop Nick and the children someplace, but he declined and hailed a cab as soon as the limo had driven off.

"You lied, Uncle Nick," Josie said, her lower lip protruding in a judgmental pout.

"It was necessary."

"But you lied to the king. Isn't that a crime or something?"

"I know this is hard for you to understand, but if I don't lie, everyone will find out that Auntie Mellie and I aren't getting along so well. And if that happens—"

"I know, the dragon-lady social workers will take me and Jakob away."

"And we'll go to the orph'nage," Jakob said almost cheerfully. Despite many assurances, he'd never let go of this notion.

Josie did not look satisfied with Nick's explanation, but he couldn't help that. Sometimes the end *did* justify the means.

AMELIA AT FIRST thought dinner would work out okay. CeCe had pulled a few strings to get them a table tucked into a corner at a new, trendy Italian eatery in the Village. Nick, who had at first vehemently objected to dinner out, had taken some convincing. But once committed, he'd pressed his slacks, put on a tie and changed shoes, instantly debonair.

He could be downright charming, too, when he wanted to be, and he devoted a lot of energy to charming the socks off CeCe and doing the male-bonding thing with Shane. No matter what topic of conversation came up, Nick could contribute something interesting to it. He seemed to know more about the shipping business than Amelia herself, even though she'd grown up with it. He also knew an almost obscene amount of trivia about New York, since he'd spent most of his time in America visiting museums and libraries, trying to force-feed culture to the children.

She was pretty sure he hadn't taken them to Coney Island.

Amelia herself said little, believing that the less she interacted, the less obvious it would be how tense she was around her husband.

"So how *did* you two get together?" Nick asked Shane and CeCe. "Amelia has only made veiled references to some rather odd circumstances."

CeCe laughed. "Business partners make strange bedfellows. Literally."

"Ah," Nick said, nodding.

"We really despised each other at first," Shane said. "But there's a fine line between anger and passion." He looked at CeCe, as if seeking approval, and she nodded almost imperceptibly.

CeCe took up the story from there. "Once we stopped arguing and started really talking, everything fell into place. It was just a matter of understanding what each of us truly wanted. And we weren't nearly as far apart as we'd pretended."

"Of course," Shane added, "the baby made all the difference in the world. We might never have worked out our differences if Easton hadn't insisted we marry."

"Even then, it was touch-and-go for a while," CeCe said, taking a dainty bite of her manicotti. "But the baby—every time I thought about it, I knew we had to find common ground. We'd created this life together, and we had a responsibility toward it. It's brought us so close, closer than I ever could have imagined being to another human being.''

Amelia was wishing she had a handy airsick bag. Was this soppy sentimentalist her hard-driving sister CeCe? Now she and Shane were staring into each other's eyes with goo-goo expressions. Apparently the rest of the world had receded for them, as Amelia and Nick had become invisible.

Amelia caught Nick's eye. His expression was as pained as hers must have been. Why did he have to be such a good actor? There were times during the evening she could have convinced herself they really were a happy newlywed couple, he'd been so damn agreeable.

She could see now, though, he was as tortured as she.

''Will you be having dessert?'' their waiter asked as a busboy cleared the table.

''No,'' Nick and Amelia said together, a bit too enthusiastically.

''Um, I've got a bit of a headache,'' she explained to CeCe and Shane. ''I haven't acclimatized back to New York weather yet.''

CeCe yawned. ''I'm tired, too. I guess those days of partying till the wee hours are over.''

''Unless you call 4:00 a.m. feedings a party,'' Shane said with a mischievous smile. His efforts earned him a sharp elbow from his wife.

CeCe's plan was painfully obvious. Hang out with Amelia and Nick and show them firsthand how blissful marriage and parenthood could be, even in a relationship that had started on very rocky ground. It almost worked on Amelia, she admitted to herself. Every time she thought about CeCe's pregnancy, her own womb contracted. She'd always wanted children, and the strong possibility that she might be doomed to a childless existence troubled her greatly.

Nick, though, wasn't buying a word of it. She could tell by the muscle that jumped in his cheek, even as he patted Shane on the back in a gesture of camaraderie and kissed CeCe's cheek as they parted company in the penthouse foyer.

"Sorry about that," Amelia murmured when the other couple was out of earshot.

"You mean your sister's not-so-subtle attempts to fix our ailing marriage?"

"I had no idea that was what she had planned."

"I had no idea it was so obvious the marriage needed fixing."

"It's not. I confess, I told her what a disaster the cruise was. I'm just not in the habit of holding things back from her. But I don't think anyone else really knows how royally pissed off we are at each other."

"Royally pissed. Now that's a good one. Shall we check on the kids?"

AMELIA WAS WRONG. Apparently *everyone* knew of the royal couple's marital tensions, and *everyone* wanted to do something about it.

Efforts continued the following day, when Lucia popped over to the penthouse with the lame excuse that she'd lost an earring and thought it might be there. Though Amelia was dutifully studying an ancient tome Easton had given her, detailing the history of the royal family, Lucia thought nothing of interrupting her. And though Amelia didn't really feel like talking, Lucia plopped down on the opposite end of the sofa on the screened lanai and took the book out of Amelia's hands.

"Talk to me."

"What do you want to talk about?" Amelia asked pleasantly.

"You know. You and Nick."

Of course. Lucia didn't have a subtle bone in her body. Whatever she was thinking came straight out of her mouth. "What's to talk about?"

"I want to know how the honeymoon went."

"Pretty much a nightmare from day one. No, that's not true. There were a few days when Nick and I got along beautifully, when he was teaching me to cook. And I got along very well with the children, part of the time."

"And when you were getting along...did you get along? You know?"

"I have no idea what you're—"

"Did you use the going-away present I gave you?"

"I've been meaning to speak to you about that. I can't believe you gave me a handful of condoms right in front of a bunch of media vultures."

Lucia laughed. "No one saw them."

"The children very nearly did."

"Oh. Forgot about that. But they didn't, so it's okay. Weren't they a scream? You did use them, I assume. Excellent."

Amelia recalled that she'd wanted to thank her irrepressible sister for providing a handy means of birth control. Otherwise, she and Nick never would have... But she didn't want to encourage Lucia's deviant habits.

"Do you need more?" Lucia asked.

"If I need more, I'll buy them myself," Amelia said, a bit more sharply than she meant to. "Your interest in my sex life is unhealthy."

"I wasn't asking for details," Lucia said huffily. "Just trying to be helpful. You've probably never bought a condom in your life."

"Will you not say that word so loud?"

Lucia sighed. "If that word offends you, I guess you don't want to see the presents I bought for you."

For the first time, Amelia noticed a foil shopping bag sitting by Lucia's feet. She knew she shouldn't, but… "What presents?"

Lucia brightened. "Wedding presents. You got married in such a rush, I didn't have time to even think what to get you, much less actually buy it."

"Nick and I requested no one give us gifts," Amelia said.

"I know, but I'm your sister. I'm allowed. Here." She reached into the shopping bag and pulled out a small box wrapped in hot-pink paper.

Amelia took it and started peeling off the paper. Knowing Lucia, it could be anything—an exquisite piece of jewelry or a knife sharpener.

The last piece of paper came free and Amelia removed the lid from the box, revealing a bottle of something pearly-pink. "Lotion?"

"Not just any lotion. Read the card."

"Scented massage lotion…heats to the touch. Oh, Lucia," Amelia scolded as she hastily closed the box.

"Don't knock it till you've tried it. A strong relationship is based on mutual trust, and massage helps build trust."

For one self-indulgent moment, Amelia allowed herself to think about using the lotion on Nick, her slick hands gliding over the smooth muscles of his back, his thighs, his…

"Thank you," Amelia said diplomatically as Lucia handed her another box. With some misgivings, Amelia opened it, then relaxed slightly. Lingerie. Every woman could use lingerie, even if it did have leopard spots and tiger strips. "Very nice."

"It's edible."

Amelia's face heated up like a brick of charcoal. "You're bent."

"I'm not. Haven't you ever read Dr. Ruth? Playfulness is an important aspect of—"

"Okay, I get the picture. Thank you so much for your…thoughtfulness."

Lucia's laughter echoed across the room. "You'll thank me someday, sister."

Amelia doubted that. She gathered up the tasteless presents and took them to her room, where she hid them under the bed behind some house slippers she never wore.

On her way back to the screened lanai to continue her studies, Amelia smelled something delightful coming from the kitchen. She found Hester and Bernice conspiring over what looked like a very elaborate dinner.

"Are we entertaining this evening?" Amelia asked. Her grandfather occasionally invited some dignitary to the penthouse for an evening, sending the staff into a tizzy of preparations.

"Oh, no, dear," Hester said. "We just felt… creative."

"What's in the oven?"

"Chateaubriand," Bernice said with a twinkle in her eye. "Along with steamed baby asparagus, rosemary new potatoes, honey-glazed carrots and a surprise for dessert.''

Amelia's newly born cooking instincts came to life. ''Can I help?''

Hester and Bernice exchanged a look. ''Your place isn't in the kitchen, dear.''

CeCe and Shane arrived home just then. ''We won't be here for dinner,'' CeCe announced to Hester as she swept into the kitchen to get a bottle of mineral water. ''Oh, you're cooking something special?''

''Just having some fun,'' Hester said.

''Sorry for not letting you know earlier,'' CeCe said. ''But Shane and I volunteered to help with a birthday party at a skating rink.'' She turned to Amelia. ''I thought we might bring Josie and Jakob with us. They'd probably like to spend time with some other children, don't you think?''

''That's a great idea.'' Amelia started to volunteer herself as another chaperon. The thought of surrounding herself with a group of noisy, messy children was very appealing. But then she remembered the special dinner. Hester's feelings would be hurt if everyone bugged out. ''I'll ask Nick, but I'm sure he'll agree. The children have spent far too much time in adult company.''

''Where is he?''

''He took the kids to yet another museum.''

CeCe frowned. ''They must be bored out of their minds.''

They drifted out of the kitchen and onto the lanai, where their conversation was more private. ''They don't seem to be bothered, actually,'' Amelia said. ''They enjoy being with Nick, no matter what the circumstances. They lap up his attention like it's elixir from the gods.''

"And what about your attention?"

Amelia didn't know how to answer that. Nick had not invited her to accompany them on their museum jaunts. He knew she had to study, and meet with the king, and do other prequeenly things, so perhaps he'd merely been showing courtesy by not tempting her to play hooky. But she felt terribly left out. She missed the children, and she missed Nick.

She really missed Nick. Even though they slept in the same room every night, they still weren't sleeping together, and they seemed to be growing farther and farther apart. She missed those first few days on the cruise, when they'd conspired over meals and he'd been so tolerant of her fumbling around in the kitchen. She missed the way he'd praised her first lumpy-biscuit efforts, even though they'd almost broken his teeth. She missed the way he would so frequently brush flour from her nose or chin.

"Those children need you," CeCe said quietly. "Children need their mother."

"I don't feel like their mother. They like me all right, but they don't love me. They're holding something back because they know I won't be with them forever."

"Nonsense. They're holding something back because that's what they're learning from their father. Children aren't normally that way. They love with all their hearts, without reservation, unconditionally."

Amelia was loath to blame anything on Nick. He was doing the best he could. "They have every right to be cautious. They've lost so much. You can't imagine what they've seen."

"I know that whatever they've seen, whatever they've gone through, love can make it better," CeCe said. "Insist on spending time with them. You can show them what unconditional love is all about. That is one language children understand."

Chapter Fourteen

CeCe's words sank into Amelia's mind, and she knew in her heart her sister was right. When Nick and the kids arrived home a few minutes later, she greeted Josie and Jakob with exuberant hugs and kisses, reveling in the way they smelled and their sticky fingers all over her clothes and hair.

"Tell me what you saw today."

"Funny pictures," Jakob said.

"The Guggenheim," Josie said imperiously. "Modern art."

Amelia could not think of a more boring place for children. "And what did you like best?"

"The cars!" Jakob answered.

Amelia raised her eyebrows.

"The Guggenheim didn't hold their attention for long, so we went to an antique-car museum," Nick explained.

That sounded a bit more entertaining to Amelia. "Was there a car you liked best?"

"The 1939 Cadillac convertible," Josie said. "When I'm—if I were a princess, that's the car I would have."

The self-correction Josie had made didn't escape

Amelia's attention. She scooped Josie up into her arms and propped her on her hip. She weighed about the same as a bag of feathers. "I happen to know, King Easton has some quite nice antique cars at the palace, including an old Cadillac convertible. When you come to visit me, I'll arrange for you to take a ride in it. Would you like that?"

Josie nodded, though uncertainly.

"Me, too!" Jakob shouted.

"Yes, you, too, Jakob. Now, would you guys run upstairs and wash your hands before you touch anything?"

They flew to do her bidding, as they normally did. Nick exchanged a look with her. "You're not making promises you can't keep, are you?"

"Absolutely not. You get the kids to the palace, I'll make it happen." She told Nick about the skating party, and he agreed it sounded like fun, though the children had already had an active day.

"They'll manage," Amelia said. "As for us, I believe we're expected to dress for dinner."

Nick frowned. "What for?"

"Hester and Bernice are knocking themselves out—chateaubriand. They say it's nothing, but I smell the king behind it. Ten to one he's dining with us tonight."

"And we're supposed to knock ourselves out, too?"

"Actually, yes. Whatever our disagreements with him, he's the king, and he's also my grandfather. We owe him our respect."

Nick didn't seem convinced, but he put on the requested clothing. Amelia put on a flowered dress, stockings and heels, and even a bit of makeup. She hadn't fancied up like this since the wedding, and it made her feel nostalgic for the days when she and Nick had been working as a team rather than adversaries.

When they arrived in the dining room, they found the table formally set with tablecloth and linen napkins, flowers, candles and china with the Korosol coat of arms. Amelia had seen these dishes before, but she didn't think Charlotte had used them since her husband had died.

There were three place settings.

"Just us and the king?" Nick asked.

"I thought Mother would be eating with us, too."

Hester bustled in, placing on the table an open bottle of red wine from the Korosol vineyards. "Your mother has a headache. But the king will be here shortly."

A headache? Next thing she knew, Charlotte would be having a case of the vapors. Couldn't she have found a more plausible excuse for skipping out?

Soon after Nick and Amelia found their chairs, Easton made his entrance. He looked very debonair tonight, in a sober blue suit, white shirt and red tie featuring tiny medallions in the shape of the Korosol coat of arms. It seemed they were being reminded of their heritage at every turn.

"Good evening," the king said cheerfully. "Nice to see you two...together." He paused dramatically, giving them the eagle eye.

Amelia took a sip of her wine. Oh, this evening had been orchestrated by the king, all right, down to the variety of flowers in the centerpiece.

"I'm a bit distressed to hear that you've been spending so much time apart," Easton went on. He shook his head when Nick tried to pour wine into his glass. "That doesn't seem healthy, or natural, for newlyweds."

Amelia cleared her throat. "I've been very busy with my studies, and I see no reason Nick should be confined here just because I am."

"I'm not a slave driver," Easton said. "Two or three hours of instruction per day is all that's required for now. But it's not really a time issue, is it?"

Hester brought a tray of salads into the dining room and served them wordlessly, then slipped out. The brief pause in conversation gave Amelia a chance to formulate her answer.

"Grandfather, you already know the somewhat peculiar circumstances surrounding our marriage. Nick and I must, of necessity, spend quite a bit of time together because of our shared interest in the children, and because of our desire to present a happy marriage to the public. But we don't need to orchestrate any further togetherness. We're quite content with the status quo."

"Are you, now?" The king raised an eyebrow. "You've been awfully quiet, Nicholas. Do you concur with your wife?"

Amelia held her breath. Of course he agreed...didn't he? But she found she had an intense interest in exactly how he answered the king's question.

Nick laid down his fork and blotted his mouth with a napkin. "Actually, no, I'm not at all content with the status quo."

Oh, dear. Amelia had an awful feeling in the pit of her stomach about what was going to come out of Nick's mouth next.

"One year ago, I married a dedicated social worker named Melanie Lacey who I thought wanted to help me raise two children in a beautiful, rural village. Now, after a series of incidents that have spun completely out of control, I find myself trapped in a New York penthouse with the future queen of Korosol, being groomed as a prince. I hate it. Every minute of it. I don't want to be a prince. I don't want my children to live in a palace. But most of all, I want Melanie back. I want her in my little house in the mountains, in Montavi. I want her in my bed."

"Nick!"

He ignored her panicked objection. "I want her to get up in the morning with me and help me milk the goats."

"You have goats?"

"I want us to ride into town on a bicycle built for two and buy bread or whatever, then come home and work in the garden. I want us to sit down at the kitchen table and plan crazy vacations every year. And I can't do any of that, because Melanie doesn't exist.

"That, Your Majesty, is my opinion on the subject. I will not divorce Amelia, because I want to secure a future for those children. I'll continue to smile in public. I'll take lessons in protocol, I'll attend boring functions. But do not ask me to be happy about what's happened to my life. That's too much."

Amelia was horrified to find tears forming in her eyes. But they were tears of anger. "Are you telling me I've ruined your whole life? If not for me, you wouldn't have those children at all. And if not for the fact that I continue to put up with your Cro-Magnon attitude, you would lose them. Maybe you ought to keep that in mind before you start hurling insults and accusations.''

Nick did not have a handy comeback. He pushed his chair from the table. ''You'll have to excuse me, Your Majesty, but my wife appears not to appreciate my company.''

''*You're* the one who said *I* ruined your life!''

''Those were your words, I believe.'' He threw his napkin on the table, stood and stalked from the room.

Amelia looked to her grandfather, hoping he might do something to salvage the situation, but he merely looked sad. ''I'm so sorry, Grandfather. We've tried to keep our disagreements private, but—''

''It's all right, child.'' He patted her hand. ''I meant only to counsel you, not bring everything to a head.''

''It's not your fault. We've been on edge for days. It was only a matter of time before we blew. I'm just sorry we did it in front of you.''

''It makes me very unhappy to see the future queen of Korosol so distressed.''

''I'll be all right.'' But she wouldn't be. Not in a million years. Because she'd realized, just now, that she loved Nicholas Standish. Despite his horrid behavior, despite his coldness toward her, despite everything, she'd fallen in love with him, with the man she knew him to be—the hero, the rescuer of children, the patient teacher, the tender, generous lover.

And he apparently despised her.

''You know,'' Easton said, ''Cassandra and I didn't start our marriage on such a smooth note, either.''

''Really?'' Her grandparents' enduring love was almost legendary. No one could remember seeing them as anything but utterly devoted to one another.

''Ours was something of an arranged marriage. Not

forced, but certainly highly encouraged…a diplomatic match that would benefit Korosol. Not many people knew this, but Cassandra was actually in love with someone else when we married.''

''Really?'' Amelia said again. She'd never heard even the hint of such a rumor.

''In public, we put on a show of devotion. But in private, we could kick up quite a scene. She used to scream at me like a fishwife, claiming I'd ruined her life.''

''Sounds familiar. How did you turn things around?''

''I didn't have to do anything, really. I quickly realized she was the woman I wanted by my side. So I just showed her, at every opportunity, my very high regard for her. Pretty soon, we realized the act we put on for everyone else's sake wasn't an act at all. By going through the motions of being a loving couple, we actually turned into one. Of course, having Byrum didn't hurt matters any.''

''Nick doesn't want more children. He doesn't want a child of his to be heir to the throne.''

''He certainly has an odd notion of what it's like to rule a country. My life hasn't been so bad.''

''I'm afraid he's adamant.''

Easton patted her hand again. ''He'll change his mind. He has to.''

Hester and Bernice entered, each of them carrying a tray loaded with delicacies. The two women stopped short when they realized one of their dinner guests was missing.

''Where is Mr. Standish?'' Hester asked.

''Headache,'' Amelia and Easton said together. ''Actually,'' Easton continued, ''I'm not feeling quite the thing myself. I believe I'll go up to my room. Hester, you don't mind bringing a tray up in a while, do you?''

"Of course not, Your Majesty," Hester said with a little curtsy that almost sent chateaubriand tumbling onto the carpet.

They all watched the king depart.

"I'm not going to sit here alone and eat," Amelia said. "You've made enough food to feed a third world country. Hester, Bernice, why don't you join me?"

Bernice looked scandalized, but Hester, more accustomed to being treated as one of the family, hardly hesitated. "Mind if I set another plate and have Quincy, too?"

"The more the merrier," Amelia said.

The four of them had a surprisingly cordial dinner, but Amelia's heart ached as she thought about saying goodbye to these wonderful people she'd known so long. It ached for the love between Hester and Quincy, who had their own dramatic, romantic history. Quincy had chased Hester across an ocean to be near her. And finally, her heart ached for Nick, who was so alone despite people all around him, because he refused to open his own heart.

NICK COULD NOT BRING himself to return to the bedroom he and Amelia shared so coolly. Instead, he went to the study, the place where he'd prepared for his wedding to Amelia. It was a thoroughly masculine room, all old wood and lemon oil and leather-bound books, a ship in a bottle, antique brass navigation equipment.

This was Drake Carradigne's lair. Though he'd

died when the princesses were only children, it seemed this room had remained in a time warp.

Nick settled into the desk chair and closed his eyes. What was wrong with him, to explode like that in front of the king? He'd always prided himself on his control. But where Amelia was concerned, it seemed he had little.

He didn't hate Amelia, though an outside observer might guess that he did. He had great admiration for her. All the work she'd done, helping the ICF with their rescue missions, and she'd done it with no hope or expectation of recognition or reward. She was in some ways completely selfless.

On the other hand, her attempts to help him had certainly backfired. If he'd had any idea she was a princess, he never would have married her in Palemeir. He would have found someone else, anyone else...

No, that was a lie. He couldn't see himself married to anyone other than Amelia.

And what about Monette?

The thought came out of nowhere, and it nearly crushed him. Over the past few days he'd hardly given a single thought to his first wife and son, the two most important people in the world to him. He'd been so caught up in the current drama, he'd all but forgotten them. When Monette and William died, he'd vowed to hold them in his heart every minute of every day for the rest of his life.

At first it had been easy. But lately he'd had to work at it, as thoughts of Amelia stole into his mind when they shouldn't, tempting him with sweet memories of their lovemaking when he should have been remembering Monette in his bed.

And the children. When he first took charge of Josie and Jakob, he found they reminded him of William in countless ways, a bittersweet comfort. Now, the reverse seemed to be true. He would call up memories of William, and automatically images of Josie and Jakob would intrude. He would think of William on his tricycle, and suddenly he would think, *I need to teach Josie to ride a bike.*

How had he come to this place in his life? From happily married soldier and father to coldhearted mercenary to having responsibility for children and a wife he'd never asked for? How the hell did he regain control?

A knock sounded on the door. He knew, even before the door opened a crack, that it was Amelia. He didn't want to see her now, not until he'd figured out some things. She probably wanted to read him the riot act for unloading on the king, of all people.

But when she stuck her head in the door, she didn't look angry. "There you are."

"How did you find me?"

"Process of elimination."

"Why did you even want to find me?"

"To see if you wanted to talk. We obviously have some…issues."

Why did she have to be like this? All sweet and nice and wanting to be friends again? He wished she would just stay mad at him. It was much easier to keep her at a distance when she was spitting at him like an alley cat.

"There's nothing to talk about. We've made our decisions."

"Then will you just come to bed? I'll let you have the bed if you want. I can bunk with Josie."

"The floor is fine." Although it might have been less painful to shuttle Amelia off to another room to sleep, some perverse part of him wanted her close. So he could torture himself, perhaps, with the folly of having let himself make love to her. How could he have ever believed that a strictly sexual relationship with Amelia would be harmless, that he wouldn't be compromising his vows to Monette?

"Then let's go. The children got home a while ago. We need to tuck them in." She held out her hand to him.

What was she doing? Why didn't she just lambaste him? He wanted to tell her to go to hell, that he'd stay up as late as he damn well pleased, in any room he chose. But he found he couldn't be deliberately cruel to her. With a sigh, he got up and walked to the door, but he didn't take her hand.

The children's bedrooms were empty, but Nick heard their high-pitched voices coming from Amelia's suite. On entering, they found both kids dressed in pajamas. They sat on the carpet, playing with some toys between them.

Amelia gasped. That was when Nick realized the "toys" weren't model cars or Legos.

"Lotion heats up to the tow…" Josie read haltingly from the back of a bottle of something pink. "…to the towch."

"Touch," Amelia automatically corrected, her voice strangled.

"And what's this word?" Josie asked, pointing to something on the back of the bottle. "Eero-tic? What's that mean?"

"Never mind." Amelia snatched the bottle away from a surprised Josie and stuffed it into a drawer so fast she could have been a magician. "You two shouldn't come into this room without permission."

"And it's wrong to snoop in other people's things," Nick added. "I've told you that before."

"Sorry," Josie said grudgingly.

"Sorry," Jakob repeated.

Amelia swiftly hugged and kissed both of them. "I'll come tuck you in."

Nick, who normally would have joined in the tucking-in ritual, begged off. He really wasn't in the mood to be reassuring and fatherly and all the other things life seemed to require of him lately. But he did seem to be always in the mood for Amelia.

He mentally closed the drawer on fantasies he shouldn't have been having, anyway. Instead of letting Amelia have the bathroom first, which he almost always did, he slipped through the door himself. He needed a shower—a cold one.

THE WEATHER TURNED cool and rainy the next day, and Jakob had a case of the sniffles, so Nick declared they would stay indoors today and forgo whatever educational experience he'd had in store. The children seemed delighted to have an unstructured day, and they immediately headed for the lanai, where they started an ambitious wooden-block construction project.

Amelia decided it was high time she made good on her promise to find Josie a tutor, so she called an agency Charlotte had recommended and made appointments to interview three candidates that afternoon.

Nick, of course, had to be in on the decision. So the two of them sat in the Grand Room, doing their best imitation of a happily married couple, and conducted the interviews.

The first candidate was young, blond and very attractive. Helene appeared to be eminently qualified, with a degree in early-childhood education from Vassar and a list of former pupils that included children whose parents were movie stars, senators and Fortune 500 CEOs. Josie seemed taken with her, and they got along very well.

"I like her," Nick said when they were alone. "Let's hire her."

Not on your life, Amelia wanted to say. She did not want such an attractive woman parading around in front of Nick when their marriage was in such a shambles. "Let's just see what the others are like."

The second one was in her sixties and had "school-marm" written all over her. Her résumé was impeccable, but she seemed to stress the word *discipline* an awful lot. Josie was polite but standoffish with her.

As soon as the woman left, Nick and Amelia looked at each other. "No way," they said in unison.

The third tutor was a man in his thirties named Paul, rather handsome in an academic sort of way. He had an impressive university background in education and child psychology. He also came from a large family, in which he'd practically raised his younger siblings.

Amelia liked him immediately, and he and Josie got along like a house on fire. He even made her laugh, a sound that was heard far too infrequently.

"We'll let the agency know of our decision in the next day or so," Nick said as they showed the man out.

"How about the next ten minutes?" Amelia said

once she and Nick were alone. "Paul has got to be the one."

"You're joking, right?"

"No, of course not. Don't tell me you prefer Bombshell Blondie."

"I believe her name was Helene, and I wouldn't be making fun of busty blondes if I were you."

"Hers is bleached."

Nick actually smiled as he followed Amelia toward the kitchen, where she intended to get a cup of tea. "I think you're jealous."

"That's ridiculous," Amelia blustered, though she knew her blush was giving her away.

"You are! You can't actually believe I'd be drawn to another woman? Haven't I got my hands full with one?"

"That's just the problem." Amelia cleared her throat. "Your hands are empty. Your arms are empty. Not to mention your bed."

"That could be remedied, you know."

Amelia's hands froze in the act of pulling a mug down from the cabinet. "I wish you wouldn't offer."

"I thought maybe you wanted me to."

She did, and she didn't. If they could just feel that closeness again, maybe it would give them a basis for working on the rest of their disastrous relationship. But it seemed so foolish to peg her hopes on physical compatibility, when she knew most men jumped in and out of bed, giving it the same degree of thought as when they put on and took off their socks.

But Nick wasn't most men. He wasn't casual about anything.

"I don't know, Nick. I'm still stuck on that com-

mitment thing. I know it's hard for men to understand—''

''I understand perfectly. Some marriages are forever. Some aren't.''

She turned quickly, surprising him. He quickly
schooled his face, but not before she saw the look of
agony there.

It was Monette again, her shadow coming between
them as it always had. As it always would. Amelia's
marriage to Nick was not a ''forever'' relationship.

The doorbell rang, then rang again.

''Where is Quincy?'' Amelia asked crossly.

''Let it ring,'' Nick said. ''We need to talk about
this.''

Amelia didn't want to talk. All the talking in the
world wouldn't change Nick's feelings for her. Anyway, she was terribly afraid that if she unlocked that
door behind which she'd kept her feelings safely
locked away, she might admit that she loved him,
which would only make everything more compli-
cated.

''I've got to see who's at the door,'' she said as
she hurried out of the kitchen, wiping away a tear.

Chapter Fifteen

When Amelia entered the foyer, the security man seemed to be AWOL, too. Where was everyone? The elevator doors opened and Lucia stepped out.

"Sorry about all that ringing," she said, dripping rain on the Persian rug. "I forgot my key, and that lunkhead security guard downstairs wouldn't let me up without an argument. He didn't believe I was Princess Lucia."

As Lucia removed her rain hat, Amelia got an eyeful of pink hair and felt a pang of understanding for the security guard's confusion. "New image?"

"What? Oh, that. It was for a party. It'll wash right out. Where's Quincy?"

Amelia shrugged. "Probably sneaking a smoke on the terrace, talking the gardener's ear off. I don't know where everyone else has gotten to. I was just going to make some tea. Want some?"

"Amelia."

Amelia stopped, turned, and really looked at her younger sister. Lucia seemed troubled. "What's wrong?"

"I want to apologize. I shouldn't have given you

any tacky gifts. It seemed funny at the time, but I didn't realize how serious—"

Amelia put a finger to her lips to hush Lucia. Nick might still be lurking around somewhere, though she suspected he'd made his escape. She didn't encounter him on the way to the kitchen. She peeked onto the lanai. The kids were gone. Maybe the three of them were doing something together.

"Anyway," Lucia said, "I wanted to give you a *real* wedding present. Maybe not even a wedding present, but just a...oh, I don't know. A thank-you-for-being-queen sort of present. I'm only now coming to realize what a huge deal it is for you, and the impact it has on your marriage."

"You've been talking to CeCe."

Lucia nodded as she pulled a pastel-wrapped present from a pocket inside her raincoat and handed it to Amelia.

Given the precedent Lucia had set with her other presents, Amelia was afraid to open it. But with a bit of goading she finally did. Inside, nestled in tissue, was the most beautiful pendant she had ever seen. Crafted of gold with silver accents, studded with precious stones, it represented the Korosol coat of arms.

Any other designer would have turned a coat-of-arms necklace into a gaudy monstrosity. But Lucia had imbued the pendant with a delicate grace, lighter than air, almost like a gold spiderweb dappled with dew. Lucia had given CeCe a brooch of similar design when she'd been named heir to the throne. Amelia had secretly envied it, even though she wasn't much for jewelry, but she hadn't envied the job that went with it.

She still didn't.

"Lucia, it's beautiful. I don't know what to say."

"You don't have to say anything. Just wear it at your coronation."

"I'd be honored." She hugged Lucia, then fastened the chain around her neck. It looked silly with her casual sweater. Both sisters laughed at the results. But their laughter was abruptly cut short by the sound of an angry male voice upstairs.

Very loud. Very angry. And very Nick.

"Oh my God." Amelia ran for the back stairs, Lucia on her heels.

"He's not yelling at Grandfather, is he?" Lucia asked, sounding alarmed.

Amelia would rather that than the alternative. Unfortunately, Easton was at the embassy today. That left only a couple of possibilities.

Though the yelling had stopped for the moment, Amelia didn't slow down. When she reached the upstairs hallway, she found the door to her suite open. Inside was a distressing scene.

Nick stood in the middle of the room, his hand curled around something square and flat, which Amelia couldn't readily identify. Josie stood a few feet away, hands on hips in a defiant pose.

Amelia went inside the room, looking at first her husband, then her daughter. "Would someone mind telling me what's going on?"

"We told her not to come in here without permission," Nick said, not exactly yelling, but not at a normal volume, either. "I told her not to snoop. She deliberately defied me."

Amelia struggled to keep her voice at a normal

level. "Nick, I don't care if she came in here and cleaned out my jewelry box, that is no excuse to lose your temper with a child."

Finally Nick looked at Amelia, as if seeing her for the first time. "I didn't lose my temper."

"Oh, no? Is that why you were screaming loud enough to bring down the whole building? Is that why your jaw is ticking, and a vein is popping out on your forehead? Because you were calm and reasonable?"

He relaxed a fraction of an inch, almost as if he were slowly waking up from a nightmare.

"Josie idolizes you," Amelia continued. "Is this what you want to teach her? And what *is* that you're holding?"

Nick immediately tightened his hold on the object. Amelia realized what it was.

"It's that picture," Josie said. "Of *them.*"

Them. Monette and William.

"He hides it," Josie continued, "but he takes it out and looks at it all the time. He thinks I don't know, but I've seen him do it a lot."

"This picture is private," Nick said, teeth clenched.

Josie looked up at Amelia, her eyes pleading for understanding. "He loves her. And him. The lady and the boy. I thought maybe if I took the picture and hid it, he would stop thinking about them and he would start to love us."

The fight went out of Nick. His grip on the picture loosened until it fell onto the carpet with a thump. He sank to the bed and put his head in his hands. "Just leave me alone," he said, his voice muffled.

"Come on, Josie," Amelia said gently. "Maybe

we better just let your uncle Nick collect himself.''
She tried to take Josie's hand, but Josie was having
none of it. She'd started something with Nick, and
apparently she intended to finish it. She continued to
stare at Nick, as if she was trying to figure something
out.

When Amelia tried again to guide Josie toward the
door, the little girl deftly ducked away. She climbed
up on the bed and crawled over toward Nick, softly,
slowly, as if trying not to disturb him.

''Uncle Nick?'' she said in a whisper.

''Josie, please…''

She put a hand on his shoulder. ''Uncle Nick, who
are they? The lady and the boy?''

Nick removed his hands from his face and put them
on his knees. He looked over at Josie. ''She's my
wife. My first wife. And my son.''

''Are they dead?'' Josie asked.

Amelia resisted the urge to tell Josie to stop. She
didn't want to bring Nick any further pain, and she
feared the questions were going to stir up his temper
all over again. But to her surprise, he answered.

''Yes. They died a long time ago.''

Josie thought about this for a moment. ''It's
hard…loving people who are dead. Because they
can't love you back. I mean, maybe they're in heaven,
and they love you, but you can't feel it.''

Josie would know about these things.

''I get mad too, sometimes,'' she said softly. ''I get
mad at Mama and Papa and Tasha, my best friend,
for dying, and I get mad about the war and leaving
home, and never seeing my friends and not knowing
what happened to my dog. But I think when I'm mad,

I'm really just scared. And I'm most scared when I...when I start to forget what they looked like.''

"You don't have pictures, do you?" Nick asked, his arm stealing around her.

Josie shook her head. "I guess it was wrong to take your picture away."

Nick leaned down and picked up the picture he'd dropped, handing it to Josie. "How about if I give it to you for safekeeping?"

"Okay," Josie said uncertainly.

"You're right, I spend too much time looking at it, thinking about the past and wishing I could change things, when I know I can't."

Josie said nothing.

"Josie, I'm sorry I lost my temper. And please believe me when I say I do love you and Jakob. More than my own life. It's just been hard for me to show it."

"Because you're afraid you won't have enough love left for the people who died. I know. When you adopted me, I was scared to love you, in case my real papa came back. But I know he's not, now. So it's okay—you can love the people in the picture *and* live people, too."

"Oh, Josie." He pulled the little girl into his arms and hugged her until Amelia feared the child's fragile bones would break. "I will try. I promise."

"What about Auntie Mellie?" Josie asked anxiously. "Will you try with her, too?"

"I will try most especially hard with Auntie Mellie." Nick looked up at Amelia, his expression hopeful. "Now, why don't you run downstairs with your aunt Lucia and find your brother? And get some cookies for yourself, as many as you want.''

''Really?''

''I don't care if you spoil your dinner all to pieces.''

Josie raced for the door, where Lucia took her hand, and the two of them headed for the stairs. It was hard to believe that mere seconds earlier she had been spouting universal truths that most adults never grasped.

''That is one amazing child,'' Amelia said, her throat thick.

''She is,'' Nick agreed, his gaze still fastened on the doorway where Josie had disappeared. He stepped through it and headed for Amelia's suite. Amelia followed. ''A year ago, she lost not just people she loved, but her entire life as she knew it. Adjusting to me calling the shots must have been incredibly difficult. But I never even saw that. All I could do was focus on my own difficulties.''

''No one expects you to minimize your losses, Nick. It must have been horrible for you.'' Amelia shut the door behind her. She sat on her bed, her hands clasped in front of her.

''Everyone loses people they love.'' Nick continued. ''You lost your father when you were just a child. King Easton has lost his sister, his wife, two of his children. I don't have a monopoly on loss, but the way I've been acting, you'd have thought I did.''

''No one blames you for mourning. Your love must have been…very deep. Very enduring.''

''Yes, it was. But there are people here and now who love me, and I've chosen to indulge in self-pity rather than acknowledge and return that love. Well, that's over now. I loved Monette and William, but they're gone. And you're here, and Josie and Jakob are here. We have the makings of an incredible family.''

If only it were that simple. ''Aren't you forgetting? I'm still in line for the throne.''

Nick shrugged. ''It's not my first choice for your career, but I've been incredibly selfish about that, too. We can adjust.''

''Are you saying you'll live at the palace?''

''Will you come live part of the year in Montavi?''

''You mean…as a real husband and wife?''

Nick held out his hand to her. ''Come here, please, Amelia.''

She did, without question. Something miraculous had happened to Nick. The river of his emotions, pent up for so long, had finally burst through the dam. He even *looked* less stiff, less controlled than he had before.

He drew her into his arms. ''I've been just about the worst sort of husband a woman could wish for. Will you ever forgive me?''

''There's nothing to forgive. Pain and fear make us act in ways we believe will protect us. I've been guilty of less than sterling behavior, too. But we can start over, Nick. We can.''

''Could you come to love me? In time?''

''Oh, Nick, I fell in love with you long ago. When we kissed at the Palemeir airport, I left a piece of my heart with you then. I don't know exactly when I fell the rest of the way—when you were teaching me to cook, maybe, or when you almost died saving Josie's life, or when we made love. I realized I had fallen hard, though, that night you let King Easton have an earful.''

"Why then?" he asked, puzzled.

"I don't know.'' She smiled, feeling giddy. ''But I do love you. And I want to stay with you, forever.'' There, she'd done it. Spilled her guts.

"What about more children?" he asked.

"I'll honor your wishes, if you don't want to raise an heir to the throne. I can designate one of my sisters, or one of their children, when they have them, to succeed me.''

"And put them through what Easton has put you through? That would be unconscionably cruel. We'll have our own heir, and we'll make sure the child is prepared for the task of ruling a country.''

Amelia thought she must be hearing things. "Nick, are you joking?''

"I wouldn't joke about a thing like this. I love you, Mellie, and Josie and Jakob need a sister or brother to spoil. Besides, I won't deny you anything you want. You're my queen.''

"Not yet. Not for many more years, I hope.''

"You'll always be my queen, now and forever.'' He kissed her, and for the first time Amelia realized he held nothing back from her. He put every bit of his heart and soul into the embrace. And she returned his feelings wholeheartedly, realizing how much she'd been missing. It was as if she'd been fractured and made whole again.

The kiss grew more heated. Amelia lost herself in it, absorbing the rush of emotions that seemed to flow from Nick, now that the dam had been broken. Suddenly it seemed important to confirm those lovely words of love with a physical act to match.

"I want you, Nick, so much."

"Like I said, I won't deny you anything." He left her long enough to lock the bedroom door. He then launched a deliberate seduction that was slow and sweet, nothing like their heated, almost frantic love-making on the *Duchess.*

He pulled her sweater over her head and tossed it aside. Her lacy bra came next, then her jeans. Somehow Nick managed to make the removal of jeans a sexy thing, grazing his fingertips over her bare thighs as he eased the denim down.

He threw back the covers on the bed, then scooped her up and deposited her gently on the mattress. He made her feel so delicate, so fragile, a rare sensation for her.

He didn't immediately join her, but stood by the bed eyeing her from head to toe while he unbuttoned his shirt.

She stretched like a cat. She could never have behaved so wantonly even an hour ago. But she now trusted Nick, completely, and she had the commitment she'd longed for.

He shed the rest of his clothes and lay down beside her, drawing her close. "Are you warm enough?"

"I'm positively steamy."

"I was hoping you'd say that."

He began a leisurely exploration of her body, using his hands, his mouth, and even his eyelashes to make her sigh with appreciation for every nerve ending she possessed. She thought about getting out the massage lotion Lucia had given her, then decided it wasn't necessary. Maybe some other time they would play. Now was the time for drawing close and appreciating the many dimensions love had to offer.

When it came time for Nick to enter her, Amelia was more than eager. Her whole body pulsed with anticipation. She pulled him deeply inside her, tensing slightly as she remembered her deflowering. But there was no pain at all, only incredible sensations that catapulted through her body like shooting stars.

They rocked together in unison, perfectly aligned both physically and emotionally, rising to a simultaneous peak that was so well orchestrated it was almost poetic. Amelia didn't know whether Nick had worked it out that way, or if it was just serendipity that they climaxed at the same time, but she didn't care. It was an experience she would never forget, no matter how many times they made love.

Afterward, she longed to revel in the afterglow. But they had other responsibilities. "Nick," she said. "We really should go down and reassure the children that we've made up and everything is fine."

He sighed. "You're right."

They found both children on the terrace with Lucia, feeding pigeons. Jakob had a cookie clutched in each hand, laughing at the pigeons as if everything was fine, while Josie delicately nibbled on a cookie of her own.

Josie's face lit up when she saw Nick and Amelia enter the terrace holding hands. "Uncle Nick, guess what? I ate four cookies!"

"Sorry," Lucia said to Nick. "Self-control has never been one of my strong suits. And the pink will wash out, so stop staring."

"It's okay with me," Nick said. "The cookies and the pink hair." He scooped up both children into his arms. "It's stopped raining. How about we all go out and do something?"

"A museum?" Josie asked, not looking too thrilled.

"I was thinking Coney Island."

Since the kids had never heard of Coney Island, they looked at Nick blankly.

"It's an amusement park," Lucia explained. "With rides and games and ice cream and swimming, and I don't know what else."

"Can Auntie Mellie come?" Jakob asked.

"You bet," Nick said. "Unless...do you have queenly things to do?"

"If I do, I'm blowing them off," Amelia said. "My family takes priority."

"Wouldn't want to be in your shoes if the king finds out you're putting his precious kingdom on the back burner," Lucia said as she threw the last of the bread crumbs to the pigeons.

EASTON WAS LOOKING forward to dinner with the family tonight. He'd heard through the grapevine that Amelia and Nick had experienced some sort of breakthrough, and he felt once again that he'd made the right choice of heir.

He stood before the dresser in his bedroom, combing his silver hair, straightening his tie. Tonight would be a real celebration. Though no one had spelled it out, tonight was about celebrating Amelia and Nick's commitment to their marriage. This would be the joyous dinner their wedding reception should have been.

As he put the last touches on his toilette, a soft knock sounded at the door. Easton strode to the door and opened it, surprised to find Amelia there—looking anything but joyous.

What now?

"Come in, dear. You look a vision."

"Thank you. You look very nice yourself. May we talk for a few minutes?"

"Of course. I always have time for you." They settled into a couple of wingback chairs. Easton cleared his throat and waited for the purpose of this visit, while Amelia fidgeted. He would have to break her of that habit, but he sensed now wasn't the time to correct her.

"I guess I should just jump right into this," Amelia said. "I don't want to be queen. I'm willing to do it if I must, and I will try my hardest to be the best ruler possible. But...I'd prefer to live a more private life."

"May I ask why? I thought you were rather keen on the idea."

"It's my family."

"But I thought Nick had come around, that he was willing to compromise. You'll forgive me for listening to servants' gossip, but I'd even heard there was talk of providing an heir."

Amelia blushed. "That is all correct. But, oddly enough, the moment Nick acquiesced to my wishes, I realized why he'd been so opposed to the idea. He would weather the public scrutiny just fine. But the children—they've been through so much trauma, so much tragedy in their young lives. There may be scars we know nothing about. Now that I'm truly their mother, I feel even more protective of them than before. I feel they would fare better growing up with more privacy, less scrutiny.''

Easton was silent. The thought of abandoning Amelia as his heir was greatly upsetting. But he could tell by the intensity of her green gaze that she felt very strongly about this. And he could see her point.

''You've invested a lot in me,'' Amelia said quietly. ''And I'll understand if you don't want to change direction at this point. If you would like, I'll withdraw the request, and we can pretend this conversation never happened. I meant what I said—I'll serve to the best of my capacity.''

It was so tempting to do just that—pretend Amelia had never requested that he release her from her responsibilities. But he did not want his beloved country ruled by a queen who was unhappy, perhaps even resentful of her duties. And he certainly didn't want any further trauma to those children on his conscience. Being a member of the royal family was tough enough even when one had been born into it and prepared from birth. With Josie and Jakob being adopted, they held a unique position. Easton couldn't guarantee that resentments wouldn't crop up, jealousies with their new sibling, if one arrived.

''Would you like to think about it?'' Amelia asked.

''No. No, my mind is already made up. Although it pains me to do so, please consider yourself... disinherited. From the throne, that is, not from anything else.''

''Oh, Grandfather.'' Amelia jumped out of her chair and threw her arms around Easton. ''I won't disappoint you anymore. We'll be a good family, a strong family, a credit to the Carradigne name, a role model for—''

''Yes, yes, I'm sure you'll give the Cleavers a run for their money. Don't look so surprised. They run American sitcoms in Korosol, too. Shall we go down to dinner?'' He stood and offered Amelia his arm.

''Delighted. Oh, Grandfather, if not me, and not CeCe, who will you choose to be your successor?''

''I believe you have another sister.''

''I guess you haven't seen the pink hair?''

''She said it would wash out.''

Easton enjoyed Amelia's look of surprise as they headed toward the door to his suite. Yes, Lucia was unconventional, and outspoken, and she needed a good deal of polish. But beneath the crazy clothes and the, God help him, pink hair, he sensed a certain integrity in Lucia, a keen intelligence, and a lot of compassion. He thought Lucia might make a very good queen indeed, with the proper guidance.

Downstairs in the dining room, the dinner guests were assembling. Amelia, who had dreamed up this dinner, had invited everyone in the royal entourage as well as the whole family and the servants. She had decreed that everyone would dress comfortably, and she'd requested a bizarre menu that included hamburgers and pizza as well as Cornish game hen stuffed with wild rice—something for everyone.

But everyone seemed to enjoy themselves. Once stomachs were filled and dishes cleared away, everyone retired to the Grand Room for old-fashioned parlor games, orchestrated by none other than Lucia. The future queen's hair, at least, was now back to its original blond, with only a trace of pink here and there.

Easton took the opportunity to take Harrison Montcalm, his most senior adviser, aside and explain Amelia's defection to him.

"This is disastrous," Harrison said. "After all the time and trouble we've gone to."

"It's not so bad," Easton said. "I've enjoyed spending time with my American family. I'm getting a whole new perspective on things."

"Yes, but you're running out of heirs."

"You're forgetting Princess Lucia."

Harrison seemed to pale at the mention of the youngest Carradigne sister's name. "Surely you're not thinking..."

"I've already decided. Lucia will be crowned queen of Korosol. But I am getting a bit weary of the Carradigne sisters' unsavory little secrets popping up and spoiling things. First CeCe's pregnancy, then Amelia's secret marriage."

"Americans can be a strange lot."

"That's why I want Lucia's background thoroughly investigated. And you're just the man to do it."

Harrison appeared stunned. "Me, Your Majesty?"

"Yes, you. Who else? You're eminently qualified. I'll expect daily reports on what you find out, until you've exhausted every avenue."

"Very well, Your Majesty." But he did not seem pleased with his new assignment, and Easton wondered why.

NICK COULDN'T REMEMBER the last time he'd laughed so much. Not since he was a child. Lucia had appointed herself entertainment director for the evening, and she had everyone participating in charades. See-ing the king try to act out *Dirty Dancing* was a sight Nick wouldn't soon forget.

Another sight he wouldn't forget was his beautiful wife, laughing until tears streamed down her cheeks. And his children, their children, giggling like normal kids, snuggling up to "Auntie Mellie" with no res-ervations. They all had good reason to celebrate. The king had allowed Amelia to escape from the future-queen hot seat so that they all could lead a somewhat normal life. She'd done it for Nick, out of her love for him and the children, and he'd never guessed he could feel such happiness.

A member of the royal guard, who'd been standing watch downstairs, brought in the *Manhattan Chroni-cle,* which apparently had just been delivered. He handed it to Lady Charlotte, who gave the headlines a cursory glance, then set it aside.

Nick had been waiting for the paper. He'd been following the story of a revolution in a small African country. Not that anything in the world could con-vince him to pick up his gun again, but he was still interested.

He picked up the paper and retired to a quiet corner to have a quick look. Then, satisfied that the situation had stabilized, his morbid curiosity led him to Krissy Katwell's "Page Seven" column.

Lucia's name immediately jumped out at him. He scanned the story, and his stomach sank as he read the words that were going to cause an uproar for Ko-rosol's new future queen. Apparently she had a few unhappy past romantic relationships, and her former fiancé, some guy named Gregory Barrett, felt obligated to blather everything he knew about Lucia, attributing the failed relationships to the fact that Lucia was "fast," along with other damning character flaws.

"No one's allowed to be a hermit."

Alarmed, Nick looked up to find Lucia herself right at his elbow, attempting to take the paper from him.

"What's got you so engrossed, anyway?" she asked. "It's your turn."

Nick tried to hide the paper from her. She would find out soon enough, but hopefully not tonight. Not when everyone was having so much fun. But her own name caught Lucia's eye, just as it had Nick's.

"Let me see," she commanded with so much force Nick suddenly found he had no trouble visualizing her as a queen. He handed her the paper, and she scanned the article, her face revealing nothing.

"What is it, Lucia?" Charlotte asked.

She turned to face everyone. "Krissy Katwell, up to her old tricks. It appears I'm the target this time. But I forbid anyone to worry about it tonight," she said, tearing the paper into shreds. "Tonight is about Amelia and Nick and Josie and Jakob. We're celebrating their happiness, and I refuse to let anything interfere with that."

Everyone applauded that decision. Everyone except a tall, distinguished-looking man whom Nick recognized as Easton's senior adviser, Harrison Montcalm. Montcalm had been a general in the army when Nick was a captain, but he was retired now. He was known to be the king's closest friend.

Harrison now stared at Lucia, and Lucia stared

right back. No one else seemed to notice the tension hurtling across the room between those two.

Now, Nick wondered, what was that about?

* * * * *

*Find out what's going on
between Lucia and Harrison
in the next installment of*

THE CARRADIGNES:
AMERICAN ROYALTY
#921
*THE SIMPLY SCANDALOUS PRINCESS
by Michele Dunaway*

*Available May 2002
at a store near you.*

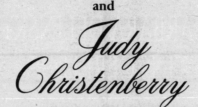

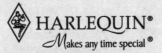

TRUEBLOOD, TEXAS

Coming in May 2002...

RODEO DADDY

by

B.J. Daniels

Lost:

Her first and only love.
Chelsea Jensen discovers
ten years later that her father
had been to blame for
Jack Shane's disappearance
from her family's ranch.

Found:

A canceled check. Now Chelsea
knows why Jack left her. Had he ever loved her, or had she
been too young and too blind to see the truth?

**Chelsea is determined to track Jack down and find out.
And what a surprise she gets when she finds him!**

Finders Keepers: bringing families together

If you enjoyed what you just read,
then we've got an offer you can't resist!

Take 2 bestselling love stories FREE!
Plus get a FREE surprise gift!

she found rice and pasta, cereal, snacks, bread and bagels, a fully stocked spice rack, flour, sugar and baking powder.

A good cook could feed an army for a month with these provisions. Unfortunately, she was not a good cook. As a relief worker for the ICF, she'd learned how to prepare beans and rice over an open fire, and in a pinch she could fry something in oil, like fish or potatoes. Most of the time, the ICF's provisions were more like field rations—tinned meats, crackers, canned fruit, all of which needed no preparation. And certainly her education had not included time in the kitchen.

There was no cookbook to be found—she supposed the professional chefs who usually worked here had all their recipes memorized.

Breakfast for seven. Cereal and milk would suffice for herself and the kids, but those four grown men would want some real food, eggs and bacon and such. That didn't sound too hard. She could probably figure it out.

She started the bacon first, laying out several slices on the built-in griddle. Soon they were sizzling nicely, the smell making her mouth water. Which made her think of coffee, which also smelled great in the morning, and which her seafaring men would no doubt be expecting.

By the time she'd found the premeasured coffee packets and figured out where to pour water into the industrial-size coffeemaker, the bacon didn't smell so great anymore. In fact, it was burning, sizzling and popping like fireworks on the Fourth of July.

Bernice had always made it look so easy.

Amelia switched off the griddle, but the bacon just